November's Past

Past

A Larry Macklin Mystery-Book 1

A. E. Howe

Books in the Larry Macklin Mystery Series:

November's Past (Book 1)

December's Secrets (Book 2)

January's Betrayal (Book 3)

February's Regrets (Book 4)

March's Luck (Book 5)

April's Desires (Book 6)

Copyright © 2016 A. E Howe

ISBN: 0-9862733-6-8
ISBN-13: 978-0-9862733-6-0

DEDICATION

In memory of Grendel—The slightly better trained, but no less goofy, inspiration for Mauser.

CHAPTER ONE

I'm a crappy detective. Oh, sorry, "investigator." I'm a crappy investigator. I never wanted to be in law enforcement. But there I was on a Tuesday morning just after dawn, looking down a highway embankment at a body.

"We got the call about forty-five minutes ago. It took us a while to locate where along the highway the guy saw it." The state trooper looked at me from under his wide-brimmed hat and decided my silence meant that I wanted to hear more. He went on telling me about the guy who saw the body, the fact that the witness was walking home from his girlfriend's place, that he had busted his phone the night before, and on and on.

The body was a white male, wearing a blue dress shirt, jeans and dress shoes. The back of the shirt was blown out and covered in blood and dirt. I couldn't walk down to take a closer look until the crime scene technicians got there to take pictures, mark evidence, collect evidence and do all the other obsessive compulsive things they do.

The crummy investigator that I was, I jumped to the conclusion that the man was probably involved in drugs, got shot by his buddies and tossed there. Well dressed, so maybe he went to buy drugs, they saw an expensive watch, tried to rob him and things went south from there. Really not a bad hypothesis.

We were only two miles from the interstate and every year a couple of bodies were dumped in Adams County, frequently from crimes committed in Tallahassee, which was in the next county over. City killers seemed to think it was clever to drop bodies out in the country. Who knew, maybe they were right. We had limited resources and not much skin in the game when it came to bodies killed elsewhere and dumped in our county. Our population was just over twenty-five thousand and our sheriff's department had only forty full-time officers. It was easy for the drug-addled to think Adams County would be a great place to dump a body.

The crime scene techs finally pulled up behind my unmarked car. I watched them make their way carefully down the embankment, photographing everything as they went.

When they finally turned the body I got my first surprise. Even from twenty feet away I could tell that he was over fifty. There aren't many people dealing in illegal drugs that are over forty, let alone fifty. It's a rough and ugly business that ravages and kills those that come in contact with it.

Drugs were probably out. Robbery seemed possible. But why move the body? You go to rob someone and it goes wrong, you just leave the body and run. Unless you want some time to pass before the crime is discovered. Maybe. Revenge? Same as robbery—why move the body? Something very hinky here.

"Large caliber wound," shouted one of the techs. "Very large. Shotgun slug maybe?"

"How long's he been dead?" I asked. "Knowing that you can't give me the exact blah, blah, blah until the coroner blah, blah, blah."

"He was killed after midnight and before four, I'd say. As a guess. Ground is wet under him so he was dumped here after the dew fell this morning. Here's a surprise." He tilted the body's head so that he could see what was left of the face. "Someone pounded this guy's face into pulp. Smashed his jaw, not many teeth left. Going to make it harder to identify him."

"Fingerprints?"

"No, the fingers are gone." He sounded a bit surprised and lifted up the stump as though he had to show me.

"Gee, thanks," I said, walking away. "Pete will be here if you need anything."

Back at the car my partner, Pete Henley, was slumped in the driver's seat, a line of drool running down his chin. I banged on the side of the car, jerking him awake.

"Jesus, Larry! Have a heart. I worked until four at the Waffle House." Pete was thirty pounds overweight and working an off-duty gig at the Waffle House wasn't helping.

"I'm going to walk up to AmMex Trucking and see if anyone there saw anything this morning. Keep an eye on the crime scene guys."

After an exaggerated sigh he said, "Yeah, okay." He seemed to think a minute and finally, unwillingly, got out of the car. Pete was okay. He just had too many irons in the fire, including a wife and two teenage daughters who wanted... well, everything.

Pete looked down the incline at the body our techs were busy processing and grumbled, "This is going to be a mess."

I walked up the road with the sun warming my back. The trucking company was only half a mile from the crime scene, but because the road curved through pine timberland I couldn't see it until I was only a thousand feet from the entrance.

"Oh, my," the middle-aged dispatcher said after I told her about the body. "Was he hit by a car? Folks drive so fast. It's crazy. Just the other day I was pulling out of the driveway—"

"This wasn't an accident," I said bluntly. It was too early in the morning for small talk.

7

"Murder?" She stared at me like I'd just told her she'd won the lottery. Only by a great force of will was she able to keep herself from picking up the phone right then and telling everyone for a thousand miles that a murder had been committed and she was lucky enough to be involved in the ultimate reality show. She'd have it posted up on Facebook before I got out of the building.

"Could you tell me who might have been coming to work this morning between four and, say, six o'clock?"

"Honey, I can do better than that. I'll just get on the intercom and ask everyone. How 'bout that?"

"Perfect."

She picked up the mic and started to speak when I noticed someone staring at me from the hallway that led back to the loading bays. As soon as I made eye contact he jumped back through a door. I started down the hall at a trot, pushing through the door into the bay where a dozen trucks were backed in.

"Who was that?" I asked an overweight man in jeans and a blue work shirt.

"Eddie. He went that way." Looking suddenly surprised that he'd answered me, he asked in a suspicious tone, "Who the hell are you?"

I opened the bi-fold that held my badge and identification.

"Oh. He ran toward the parking lot."

"Thanks."

People run from cops for any number of reasons. I turned around and went back to the front desk. I was not about to go chasing someone when I could calmly walk back over to the dispatcher and get his name, social security number and home address.

His name was Eddie Thompson. Hearing that, I cringed a little inside. The Thompsons were one of the biggest families in the county. Close knit and strange. Some of them were in local law enforcement—one of our deputies was a Thompson and so were two of the Calhoun city police.

Other parts of the clan were constantly in and out of jail on various offenses. Of course a lot of folks would tell you that a cop and a crook are just opposite sides of the same coin. Might even be true if the reason you got into law enforcement was for the adrenaline rush or you couldn't think of anything else to do.

Having radioed in a pick-up order for Eddie, I talked to a dozen people who'd come into work that morning past the body dumpsite. Nothing. There were a couple drivers who had already left on runs so I wrote their names and numbers in my notebook. Yes, I'm old fashioned that way.

I walked back to the crime scene and found the CSU guys finishing up. One of them nodded to me as I passed him. "You can go down there now."

I thanked him and looked over at Pete, who was slouched against the car reading something on his phone. No sense bothering him. I turned and started down the slope.

For me, death had an unreal quality to it. Maybe I'd seen too many horror movies. With the face smashed into an unrecognizable pulp and the hands mutilated, the body of my John Doe seemed even more like a prop on the back lot. Of course there'd been nothing in his pockets. When someone goes to the trouble of chopping off fingers and destroying dental work, they're unlikely to leave a driver's license on the body. So all I had to go by was his clothes and what was left of the body.

The clothes looked like they had been clean and fairly new before he was murdered in them. I looked at the bottoms of his shoes—barely worn and expensive looking. The man was certainly not a vagrant. His dress shirt had a button-down collar, but no tie. His belt was of high quality leather. My hopes of identifying him were going up by the minute. Middle-aged, upper-middle-class guys got reported missing. All the killer, or killers, had done was postpone the inevitable.

"What's it look like?" Pete yelled down to me.

"A very dead body. Climb down here if you want to see it."

"I'm good."

"This guy is going to be missed."

"Nice. I'll put the call out for a missing white guy."

"Tell them he's forty-five to sixty-five." I looked at the body. "Approximately 5'10" and…" He had a bit of a pot belly. "Two hundred and ten pounds. Thinning blond hair." I turned the head and looked at the eyes. "Blue eyes." From the estimated time of death, he couldn't have been killed too far from here. "Either visiting the area or lives within two hundred miles."

After climbing back up to the road, slipping twice, I told the coroner's assistants that they could take the body. I took one more look around the side of the road to see if there was any evidence that the other vehicles hadn't obliterated, then we headed back to the office.

CHAPTER TWO

I grabbed a coffee and had just settled down at my desk to check emails and read the news when I got a text: *Remember you're watching Mauser tonight.*

Damn, I'd forgotten about that. And Dad texted me instead of calling me because he didn't want to hear me complain. Fair enough. I'd told him I'd do it.

"What's up, Junior?" came a voice from behind me.

"Nothin', Deputy Dud, you?" I said without turning.

"Har, har." Matt Greene sneered as he sat on the corner of his desk and stared at me.

He was a good investigator with moments of greatness, but as a person he was a little shit. At 5'5" he was the shortest man in the department and only one of the women was smaller. He usually worked alone. No one wanted to spend a minute more around him than they had to. He had been married once. She attempted suicide and then moved to the other side of the country. I'd even heard deputies say that if he called for assistance they'd drive very slowly. Maybe his badass personality worked for him. Suspects didn't want to be around him any more than his fellow officers and were quick to tell him everything they knew just so they could go to a cell and be around decent criminals.

"Heard you got a body." There was irritation in his voice. He thought he should be lead on every homicide.

"Yep." Give him nothing was my motto.

"Must be nice being the boss's son."

"Has its perks." I was scrolling through missing persons, wishing he'd go away but knowing he wouldn't.

"Who's the victim?"

I turned in my chair. "What are you working on?"

"Arson. Happened last night. Pretty interesting." The only trick I knew of to deal with Matt was to ask him about his cases. When he started talking about an investigation it was as though he shifted gears from asshole to insightful. "I've been going over it with the fire chief. Still smoking, but we were finally able to do a walk through an hour ago." He was also notorious for being able to go without sleep.

"Interesting how?" I asked casually.

He narrowed his eyes. "Why do you care?"

"Never know, I might hear something on the street."

"You on the street, that's a good one. Your dad moved you to CID after what, barely two years on patrol? Faster than anyone else." He was back to being an asshole.

Don't go on the defensive, I had to remind myself. "Screw you." I turned back to my computer and Matt went on about his business.

Half an hour later I'd gone through all the regional missing persons that matched our dead guy's stats. Nothing.

Pete was just wandering in.

"Heard anything?" I asked him. I'd dropped him off at his usual morning haunt. Every day that we didn't have a nuclear attack or something more urgent, he would spend at least an hour at Winston's Grill, eating as many eggs and pancakes as he could get on his fork and over his tongue.

"No, everyone was askin' me about it." His hour at the grill on county time was not money wasted. Pete knew everyone and everyone knew Pete. His finely tuned ears picked up every bit of gossip and whisper of scandal that blew through town. Dozens of felonies had been cleared off the books by information that he got yakking with diners. People loved to talk and he was the perfect listener. Because of that he knew more about the county and the people in it, past and present, than anyone else.

"Sylvia Foster is hanging out with some guy from up north, but he sounded too young to be our victim. Might be worth a look as a possible suspect." Pete dropped down into his chair.

I sent emails to all police and sheriffs' departments within a hundred-mile radius of Adams County. Sending out general calls for information was fine, but poking the right people was a lot better. Then a burglary call came in. There were eight of us in the criminal investigation department, which meant there weren't enough of us to specialize. We all grabbed cases as they came while the major violent crimes were assigned individually by our supervisor, Lt. Johnson, or the sheriff, who just happened to be my father. I took the burglary and headed out to interview the victims.

I spent an hour at a small ranch house on a dirt road in the south of the county, talking with a stoop-shouldered man and his wife about the TV, electronics and a jar of quarters stolen from their house while they were at a funeral. I stood silent while the old farmer shed tears, explaining that his son was an addict and he believed he was responsible. This was one of the reasons I didn't want to be an investigator. There was no way to make this right.

The mother explained that her son had been injured doing construction work, got hooked on pain killers, then followed meth down the rabbit hole. They wanted us to arrest him so he could detox in the county jail where he'd be looked after by a doctor. What a sad commentary on our world that parents needed their son to be locked up in order to get medical and psychiatric care.

Back at the office, Pete told me about a stolen car report he'd just taken.

"The usual—some guy gave his keys to a woman at the Eldorado Bar so she could get some aspirin out of his glove box. Of course she drove off with the car and tried to trade it for drugs, etc., etc." He was just finishing the report. "We already found the car, so the idiot will get it back. Lesson learned, not." He pounded away at his keyboard.

While he was talking I noticed that the arson report was sitting on Matt's desk, very much unattended. There was no rule in the department that said we couldn't help each other out on cases. No one had ever said we had to ask the lead investigator if he wanted any help. I opened the file and took pictures of it with my cell phone. No one noticed. I thought maybe I could have some fun looking over Matt's shoulder on this one.

I finished up by writing up a report on an assault case. After sending it to our lieutenant I glanced at the clock. *Crap.* I only had about an hour before I had to go to Dad's house and babysit Mauser. I left the office and grabbed a quick dinner on the way, not really looking forward to the rest of the evening.

CHAPTER THREE

I pulled through Dad's gate and up the gravel drive to his small house. It sat on twelve acres surrounded by woods. Dad kept a couple of horses that he rode in parades and when directing searches with the mounted posse. He tried hard to be the very picture of a sheriff.

I was greeted at the door by... nothing. I walked down the hall. "I'm here!" I shouted.

A gruff *woof*, deep and low, came from the living room. The "baby" I was there to sit. Lying on the dirty sofa was the one-hundred-and-ninety-pound, two-year-old Mauser. Black with white markings and floppy ears, the Great Dane looked up at me from under hooded eyelids.

"Yeah, it's you and me tonight, boy-o," I told him. He closed his eyes and stretched out his legs.

"He's had his dinner," Dad said as he entered the room while adjusting his coat. He stood a little shorter than my six foot even. His grey hair was cut short over his square head, illuminated by green eyes that penetrated bad guys, deputies and voters—basically anyone that he wanted to control. Those eyes were Sheriff Ted Macklin's superpower.

"What's this?"

"Thirty-fifth high school reunion. I told you all about it."

"Right. And how long do I have to babysit the monster?" Mauser moaned as though he understood me.

"Hey, don't hurt his feelings," Dad said, only half kidding.

"You know, if you had trained him when he was younger you wouldn't have to have a babysitter for him."

"He has a free spirit."

Dad had no idea how to train a dog. We'd had Great Danes when I was growing up, but it was my mother who trained them. Dad trained me. That was the division of labor between my folks. Clearly Dad was a failure at raising kids or pups.

"I boarded over the hole in the dining room wall."

"He got out again?" Mauser had dug through the wall, making his own doggy door when he was just six months old. Whenever he was unattended and bored he simply dug through the drywall and went outside.

"The kid I've got taking care of him in the afternoons was late." My dad placed the blame for the huge hole in the wall squarely on the boy. "I've put the padlock on the refrigerator. The keys are in the drawer next to it." Mauser could open the refrigerator like a pro if it wasn't locked.

"Yeah, yeah, go. I'll take care of the beast." The beast looked unimpressed with my bravado.

"He gets a snack at eight, his walk is at nine and his final bedtime snack at eleven, but he probably won't want to go to bed until I get home. Just go ahead and give him his bedtime snack. If I need to, I'll give him another one when I get home." Dad frowned as I dramatically rolled my eyes. "I'll be back by one o'clock. If I have a lady in tow, just sneak out the back door."

"Like that's going to happen."

"Back at you, Romeo." He patted his pockets for keys, pulled them out, spun away on his cowboy-booted heels and left me with the oversize lap dog.

"Remember, I'm not a softy like your dad," I told the couch weight.

Checking my phone, an email told me that a preliminary autopsy report wouldn't be done on my victim until tomorrow. So with nothing to keep me out of trouble, I transferred the photos of Matt's arson file to my iPad so I could check it out. Maybe with a little luck I could solve it before him.

The fire had started in the middle of the house. A small amount of accelerant was used, but not much was needed. It was an old house and built out of heart of pine. Once the fire got a taste of that fat pine the flashover happened in the first ten minutes and the house was a lost cause by the time the fire department got there.

Motive. That was the big question. Maybe it was a firebug just getting his jollies. Possibly. They usually try not to hurt anyone, so an abandoned building that was not being used by squatters would fit the bill.

Mauser was just finishing his evening snack when I decided I wanted to drive over and take a look at the arson scene.

"Hey, you." Mauser turned and gave me a suspicious look. "Want to go for a little drive?" I had his full attention now. "Come on."

I had to use Dad's ratty old minivan since Mauser didn't fit in my car. Dad had removed the middle seats of the van to give Mauser a large area behind the front seats to stretch out. Mauser took full advantage of his position as backseat driver by drooling over my arm and huffing into my ear whenever he saw something interesting. Between the dog smell and the fact that the van had a large "Ted Macklin for Sheriff" sign on the side, it pretty much sucked as a joy ride vehicle.

"You know, you're going to have to grow up on your own," I told Mauser as we traveled through the night toward town. "Dad isn't going to give you the proper training. If you want to stay out of trouble, you've got to learn to control your impulses."

He put his head on my shoulder and drooled down my

chest. I gave up. Mauser would have to solve his own problems growing up with Dad just as I had.

I slowed down as I approached the location of the arson. The burned-out house was in an older section of Calhoun known as Deep Water, with medium-sized homes on large lots, most of them built at the turn of the last century. I was going to park in the driveway, but it was filled with boards and other crap that the fire crews had pulled from the house, so I parked at the curb.

As I stepped from the car I looked around to see what other houses might have a view of the crime scene. There were three houses across the street that could see the driveway and the house. The houses on either side had too much shrubbery and trees between them to be able to observe anyone coming or going. Most of the homes in the neighborhood still had their lights on as families settled in for the night.

I took out my flashlight and headed up the drive, leaving Mauser to guard the van. For him, "guarding" involved lots of heavy sighs and lying down out of sight.

The yard was well kept for an empty house. The lawn was mowed and the hedges in the front looked like they had been trimmed this summer. My flashlight illuminated the blackened structure. There wasn't much left except for parts of the walls. Looking through the charred windows, I could see that the house still had lots of furniture in it.

A loud *woof* sounded through the quiet neighborhood followed by an even louder "Shit!" I trotted back out to the van to find an older gentleman holding his chest and shaking.

"You okay?"

Mauser gave out another bark as though I'd asked after his health.

"Not you, you big idiot."

"I'm fine. He just scared the holy ever-loving crap out of

me." The man was still holding his chest and breathing hard.

"You sure you're okay?" I really didn't want to have to call an ambulance for him.

"Fine," he said, straightening up and smoothing back the wispy strands of white hair that surrounded a sparsely populated dome. "Just came over to see who was poking around the Daniels place."

I pulled my bi-fold out and showed him my badge as best I could in the light from my flashlight. "I'm Deputy Larry Macklin."

"I figured that out seeing as this is your daddy's van." He looked at the van. Mauser stared back out at him. "And his horse," he said gruffly, clearly not having forgiven Mauser for the fright. "I've known your dad since he was a teenager."

"And you're…?"

"Sorry, I'm still recovering. Tom Canfield." He held out his hand. I switched my flashlight to my left hand and shook with him.

"They know who did this?" Canfield asked, sounding sad and puzzled.

"It's early days."

"I thought someone else was in charge? Some guy named Greene, I think."

Awkward. "Small department. We all have to pitch in," I said, wanting to leave it vague. "Just thought I'd help out."

"Oh, okay."

"Did you see anything?" I pointed toward the burned-out house.

"No. Told the other deputy the same thing. I'm not one of those neighbors who sticks their noses into other people's business." He realized that coming to check me out seemed to put the lie to that. "Of course, with the fire and all, I'm keeping a closer eye on what's going on in the neighborhood. Guess that's closing the barn door after the cows got out."

"Still a good idea. Crime scenes can attract some

unsavory characters." I made a small joke at my expense. "Do you think anyone else might have seen something?"

"Doubt it. Only real nosey barker in the area lives over on the street behind me."

I let that one go. I didn't need to hear a grievance list against a neighbor that couldn't help with the investigation.

"Why has the Daniels house been empty?"

"Well, Mr. Daniels died and his wife, Susan... Well, she was getting pretty dotty. Her daughter took her back to wherever she lives. Tennessee, I think. Maybe it's Georgia."

"When did she move out?"

"Look, my hip can't take all this standing." I thought he was going to bug out on me, but he surprised me. "Why don't you come over to my porch where we can be more comfortable?"

Once we were seated on wicker chairs and his wife had fetched us both a glass of tea, we got back on track.

"Susan moved out two, maybe three, years ago. I've just been happy they hired Jack's to mow the grass and keep the place looking decent." Jack's was the most reputable of the lawn services available in the county.

"Any reason you can think of for someone to burn the house down?"

Canfield shook his head. "No. The Danielses had lived there for almost as long as I've lived here. Never made no enemies. Raised two girls. One a lot nicer than the other. That's Dell. She's the one that took her momma to live with her."

Could the cost of keeping the house up be a good enough reason to burn it down?

"I thought they might try and sell it. But I guess it means something to them. Dell was acting like her mother might be able to come home. I knew that was wishful thinking. But from what Susan used to say, Dell and her husband have plenty of money."

There went that motive.

"You don't look much like your dad."

I took this as a compliment. "Guess I take after Mom."

"I was sorry to hear about her. I met her a couple times. Real sweet."

"She was the sweet to Dad's sour."

"Ah, now, your dad's all right. He used to hang around the Daniels place."

"Really?"

"Yeah, that was back when he was a teenager. High school. Must have been the late seventies."

This was an odd turn. "Why was he hanging around over there?"

"Ha, ha, the girls! Both of them were nice looking. A year or so apart. I don't know which he was more interested in. I didn't pay much attention back then with work and all. Our boy was a little older so he didn't run with that crowd. But there were always kids hanging out over there. Playing football in the yard and smoking when they thought they could get away with it."

He was clearly lost in days gone by. I didn't really know how any of this could help, especially that part about my father, but I was always fascinated to hear about the gruff ogre's younger days.

"They'd ask for help sometimes. I think your dad, or might have been one of the other boys, got his truck stuck one time. Just things like that."

A couple more stories and I could tell that he was getting tired. I stood up. "Thanks, Mr. Canfield, it was a real pleasure talking to you."

He took my hand again and shook it vigorously. "Same here, young man. But tell your dad to keep his damn horse at home." He laughed at his own joke.

In a few minutes I was headed back to Dad's house. "Well, Mauser, what'd you think about all that?"

He butted my head with his and flung slobber down the side of my face.

"Let me guess, ice cream? You really think you deserve a treat for barking at that old man?"

He bumped my head again—a clear answer. "Fine, Buster's it is."

It was only a slight detour to get him a cup of vanilla and a waffle cone for myself. Mauser is well known at Buster's and the woman working the window greeted him by name. She asked where the sheriff was, but didn't seem to remember me from the half dozen times I'd come by. *That's life in the shadow of my dad and his dog,* I thought.

CHAPTER FOUR

Half an hour after midnight Dad came through the door looking tired. Mauser greeted him with a couple of loud barks and gently taking his arm in his mouth. Dad patted the side of Mauser's head and ruffled his ears.

"My God, it makes you feel old hearing about everyone's illnesses, their grandchildren, divorces and dead spouses." He sat down on the couch and Mauser got up beside him, dropping his head into his lap.

"Did the boy treat you all right?" he asked the Dane, scratching him behind his ears.

"I even got him ice cream," I said without thinking where it might lead.

"Why'd you go out?"

To get the dog ice cream would not have been believed. "I drove over to one of your old haunts."

"How's that?" I'd piqued his interest. Probably not the best idea.

"The Daniels house. The fire last night."

"The arson. I didn't realize it was their house. Knew it was close. Isn't that Matt's investigation?" His eyes narrowed. He was paying full attention now.

"It is. I just thought I'd take a look at it."

"Bullshit. You don't take on extra work for the fun of it. Did he ask you to look at it?" He didn't give me a chance to answer. "No. 'Cause he doesn't like you. You don't like him. So knock it off."

He'd worked himself into a mood. He was always quick to anger and even quicker to anger when he was tired. Time to change course.

"So you were hot on one of the Daniels girls?"

"Where the hell did you hear that?" he asked with more puzzlement than anger. Redirection was the best method to use on Dad.

"Talked to a fellow who lives across the street. Tom Canfield. Said that you used to hang out over there. He thought it was something to do with the girls."

"Margret and Dell..." He got a wistful look on his face. "Margret was prettier, but had a mean streak. Dell would do anything for anybody. Both of them moved out of the area years ago. Margret was in my class. I kinda wondered if she'd be at the reunion tonight. Funny. Thinking about her for the first time in years and I come home and you bring her up."

"So you had a thing for her?"

"I went out with Margret once. But that temper of hers ruined the evening. She stormed out of the theater and I spent an hour looking for her. High maintenance, for sure. Your mother was more my speed. Easygoing country girl. Margret married Jim Devries... You met her a few times when you were younger. 'Course, they've been divorced for years."

I hadn't realized that Margret Devries was Margret Daniels. I vaguely remembered her from trips with Dad to Mr. Devries's farm. She'd never seemed like a farmer's wife. I guess she wasn't.

"Mr. Canfield made it sound like you spent a lot of time over there."

"Not that much. But it seems like there was always a lot of drama around the Daniels house. Somehow that equated to excitement to us small town kids. There was a group of us. The two Daniels girls. Jim Devries. Fred Chandler. Fred died ten years ago in a car accident. Anyway, those were the regulars and then there were always a couple more girls or guys hanging out too. Margret and Dell's parents both worked so we could get away with a little more there. Most of the rest of us had a mom or dad who was home after school."

Dad's mind returned to the present. He looked at me. "House burned down. That's a shame. It was empty, right?"

"Yeah, Mrs. Daniels was the last one living in the house and, according to Mr. Canfield, Dell came and took her home to Tennessee or Georgia so she could take care of her."

"A lot of the folks at the reunion are taking care of their parents. Wish my folks were still around, but I'm glad neither of them suffered long. Who could have burned down the house?"

"That's what I was looking into."

Wrong thing to say. "Well, knock it off. Leave it to Matt." He eased Mauser's head out of his lap and stood up. "I'm serious, stay away from that case."

That did it. Having Dad tell me no just made me more stubborn and more determined to keep an eye on the arson case.

At noon on Wednesday I got a text from the coroner: *Something you might want to see before we send the body to the morgue.*

It was a great excuse to go for a drive. Our community was too small for its own hospital, so our coroner did his work out of a hospital in Tallahassee, about thirty-five minutes away. The leaves were changing and the weather was cool and dry. I rolled down the windows and lived for the moment.

Dr. Darzi was sewing up the giant "Y" incision in the victim's chest as I came in.

"Ahh, good. Just in time." His Indian accent and

complexion were light. Not more than forty years old, he was a good-looking man with the confidence of one who is seldom wrong.   We had met half a dozen times over victims: two or three car accidents, at least one stabbing and a gunshot.

"Come here, come here." He waved me over. "Put some gloves on and help me turn him."

I looked around to see if there was an assistant he was talking to. No one. He pointed to a box of plastic gloves. I didn't mind looking at a dead body, but I wasn't thrilled about the idea of touching one.

We awkwardly rolled the body over. Darzi waved his hands toward the victim's ass and smiled wide. Reluctantly, I looked. There on the dead man's right butt cheek was a tattoo about the size of a playing card. It was a quality piece of work, reading in gothic scroll "Kiss My Ass." Now I smiled. A piece of art like that was going to make my job easier.

"Nice," I said, inspecting it closer.

"A quality tattoo," he said. I pulled out my phone and took a couple of pictures. He continued talking. "You're lucky he was lying face down. The lividity. The blood went to his belly and not his backside."

"Nothing from the teeth?"

"The man didn't have any major dental work. Only a couple fillings. No good. And the assailant did a damn good job smashing up his teeth. Would be very hard to get a comparison with X-rays taken before the assault. Unless we were reasonably sure who it was… Then the teeth and the little bit of work might be able to confirm his identity." He shook his head and shrugged. "I took palm prints… Not likely to help much without the fingers." He held up his hand and wiggled his fingers as though I might not know what he was talking about without his own digits as examples.

"Death was most likely caused by the massive chest wound which in turn was most likely caused by a slug fired from a twelve-gauge shotgun. Powder marks on the skin suggest that the shotgun, if it was a shotgun, was fired from a couple of feet in front of the victim."

"What was used to smash his face in?"

"Standard carpenter's hammer, most likely. I took 3D images to use if we find a weapon. Also, I sent all the images to a forensic artist. However, they might need the skull in order to do a complete reconstruction and rendering of what he looked like before someone went all Thor on his face." He shrugged again. "Anyway, the artists are very backed up so it will be a couple of weeks before you'll get anything back."

I was trying to think how I was going to convince the Florida Department of Law Enforcement to pay for the forensic artwork. The state had deeper pockets than Adams County did. Dad would grumble for a week about lab money spent on an out-of-county victim.

"How far do you think he was transported after death?"

Darzi looked up and seemed to be making calculations in his head, but I knew that this was a ruse. He was perhaps the most meticulous professional I'd ever met. I was sure that he'd already thought of and made his guestimates before I arrived. He always dictated thorough notes for an assistant to type up before closing up the body and sending it to the morgue.

"Not much more than an hour. I'd say he was shot, dismembered and defaced, then quickly moved to a vehicle where he was placed in a face-down position and finally shoved down the embankment. All in under an hour."

Armed with the tattoo pictures, I decided to visit a couple Tallahassee parlors to get a professional's opinion of the work.

At the first parlor half a dozen tattoo artists gathered around and commented on the pictures. The gist of it was that the work had "crisp lines, good color contrast, intricate and unique lettering." If done locally it would run about a thousand bucks. One interesting comment was that the guy had taken good care of it after the work was done.

After they had hemmed and hawed over it for a while, I was directed to another shop in town to speak with Erick. According to the first crew, he had an almost encyclopedic memory for styles and might be able to tell me who the artist was, or at least where it might have been done. The "where" part of it could be a lot harder than I thought, because they all started speculating on what country it might have been done in. An overseas tattoo parlor had never crossed my mind.

I met with Erick, a giant with a Viking beard and hairstyle. He took one look and said it was very similar to work that a girl in New Orleans was doing. He didn't know her last name but she went by Dahlia, and he was able to give me the last place he knew she had been working. He shook my hand with an enormous bear paw that left me wondering how he could possibly manipulate a tattoo needle with any precision.

Back in Calhoun, I had to deal with a few reports before I could follow through on the tattoo lead. Nothing much—a smash-and-grab that netted the perp thirty bucks and a bar fight with the victim already wanting to drop the charges. Phone calls to the officers who took the reports told me everything I needed to know. The thirty bucks was filed away in the "if something else happens that might make this important" drawer. The assault was going to require me to do some more interviews. Other folks had witnessed it, so it was not in the power of the victim to make it go away. Depending on what everyone else might have to say, it would probably remain a decision for the State Attorney whether to pursue charges or not.

Finally I had time to check with Google and discover that the New Orleans tattoo shop still existed and had a phone number. A call told me that Dahlia worked there, but was off looking for a new place to live because she'd been evicted blah, blah, blah. I interrupted and asked for an email address to send the pictures. and said that I'd call back tomorrow if I hadn't heard from Dahlia before then.

I made a quick stop at the store on my way home. Home for me was an old mobile home on twenty acres. The property was a mix of oaks and pines with a small creek running across the western edge. My twenty acres had been part of a much larger farm before it was broken up and sold. The mobile home had belonged to the farm's foreman. The house wasn't much; I'd bought it for the land. Someday I hoped to build a cabin between four ancient live oaks. I always wondered if they had been planted there, as they formed an almost perfect square. All four of the trees were a couple hundred years old. Knurled and knotted, they were all over twelve feet in circumference. The largest was almost fourteen feet around.

I was met by Ivy crawling out from under the front porch steps, meowing for her evening meal. I let her in, trying to open the door, carry the groceries and not step on her toes. The tabby cat had been living rough in the parking lot of the sheriff's office before I adopted her. Even the burliest of deputies would feed her scraps from their lunch when they thought no one was looking. I took pity on her, bringing her home with me one especially cold night last winter. She'd never left.

We settled on the sofa after dinner. I scratched Ivy's back while I read emails and checked my social media obligations. The investigators took turns being on call and I had the eleven-to-seven shift that night. Most of the time it just involved answering a deputy's questions over the phone, but every once in a while you'd get called in to a crime scene.

I drifted off for a nap with Ivy kneading my chest. Three hours later I woke with a dry mouth from snoring and a stiff back from not moving. Ivy jumped down, perturbed that I was trying to get up. Then my phone rang. Still fuzzy-headed, I flailed around until the annoying ringtone led me to it.

"Hey, Deputy Sykes here. I knew you were on call this evening so I thought you might be interested in knowing that we picked up your runner from the trucking company."

Who? I thought. *The trucking company!* "Oh, yeah, right. Great." I really wasn't that interested. I had done a background check on him and he had a record for a dozen petty offenses. Just the type of guy to run when he sees a deputy show up at his job. No doubt he was running some small-time scam out of the place. Maybe drugs. "I'll talk to him tomorrow. Thanks."

"Yeah, well, I also got a guy here that says he saw a murder and can point me to the crime scene. That's why I called."

"You kind of buried the lead. What did he see?"

"Said he saw a guy shoot another guy with a shotgun."

I was wide awake now. "When?"

"Two nights ago."

"Where are you?"

He gave me a location about ten miles away. "Fine, I'll be there in twenty. Just let him sit and I'll question him when I get there." Sykes was not the sharpest tack in the drawer. I didn't want to take the chance of him confusing the issue.

CHAPTER FIVE

A large, older black man stood smoking a cigar next to Sykes's car.

"I'm Larry Macklin," I said as I held out my hand. He looked at my hand, a little surprised, but then threw the cigar down. After stepping on the glowing stogie he took my hand and shook it.

"Leon."

"Nice to meet you, Leon. Sykes said you saw a shooting?"

"Yeah." He sighed and looked down at the ground.

"Want to tell me about it?"

"Ha, no. But I got to."

"Why's that?"

"Saw it two nights ago. Two white guys, one shoots the other. I thought, hell, that ain't none of my business. But I haven't been able to forget about it."

"I can tell you're a good man, Leon. Makes sense that you see something like that, you can't forget it."

"Yeah, well, I hope this doesn't bite me in the ass."

"You're doing the right thing. I give you my word I'll do what I can to make sure you don't have any trouble from this." Reassuring people was half the job. Not breaking their

31

trust was the other half.

He looked unconvinced, but determined to get it off his chest. I pressed on. "Exactly when and where did you see this shooting?"

"Around midnight two days ago, Monday. They was arguing at the old warehouse by the tracks. That big old white one you can see from Jefferson. I seen one of the men point the gun at the other and shoot him right in the chest. Man dropped to the ground."

"Where were you?" I had taken out my pen and pad and was trying to take notes in the light from the street lamp.

"I was walking down Jefferson."

"What were you doing walking around at that time of night?" I didn't want to sound accusatory, but I had to get the complete story.

"I'd had a few beers at home. I live a couple blocks back from Jefferson. I wanted some smokes so I was headed up to the Fast Mart. It closes at one on weeknights."

He'd been drinking, which wouldn't help if we ever got as far as the witness stand. "But you weren't drunk?"

"Noooo. But I deliver for Southern Chips. I don't take any chances where my license is concerned."

"I hear that. So what made you look over and see these men?"

"There was a car. SUV with its lights on. I looked over and saw two white guys facing each other."

"How far away were you?"

"Seventy-five yards… no more than a hundred."

"You sound pretty sure."

"I was a spotter in the army. Got so I could judge distances pretty good."

Military, full-time job—those facts would help offset the few beers he'd had.

"Could you describe the men?"

"Not really. The glare from the headlights and the distance made it pretty darn hard to see them very well."

"Anything? Tall, short, fat, thin."

"One was taller than the other. The shooter was a little taller than the other guy. I think their hair was light colored, but that was maybe 'cause of the glare from the headlights."

"Clothes?"

"Nothing special. Shirt, pants, about the same for both." He was looking into the distance and trying hard to remember.

"What did the shooter do after he killed the guy?"

"He looked around. I put my head down and started walking fast. I doubt he could see me 'cause of the fact he was standing in the light from the car. When I got over the tracks I looked back to make sure he wasn't going to come after me."

"What'd you see?"

"Lights were off on the car, but it hadn't moved. I thought about calling the cops when I got to the store, but I didn't want no trouble. Didn't seem to be any of my business."

"What kind of car was it? Can you think of any details about it?"

"No, the lights made it too hard to see. Just big, guess it was dark colored, but the light…" He shrugged.

Sykes had left on a call while we were talking. Leon and I rode over to the warehouse. Being careful not to tread on the crime scene, I got him to point out where he had seen the two men and the car while I made notes.

Blood on the pavement was all I needed to see to call in the crime scene unit. Marcus Brown and Shantel Williams, two of our most skilled crime scene technicians, arrived first. They looked things over and called FDLE, which has much better equipment, for assistance. I left them to set up the perimeter and wait for the state folks. I dropped Leon off at his house, telling him that we'd be in touch and not to worry about any repercussions from being a witness. He looked unconvinced.

It was one-thirty by the time I got back to the warehouse and the state van pulled up just as I was parking. Marcus and Shantel had done a good job of figuring out and marking the site of the shooting. So while the four guys from the state started setting up lights, the three of us looked through the abandoned warehouse. Old machinery designed for God knows what lay at odd angles as though dropped by a giant who had gotten tired of playing with his toys.

"Keep an eye out for any place that looks like it was cleaned. Or where something was moved," I said.

Shantel, a middle-aged mocha-colored woman with broad hips, an infectious smile and eyes that could burn you down to the ground said, "Thank God you told me that, this being my very first day on the job, sir." The sarcasm dripped off her words, but she was smiling as she said it.

"I know you know what you're doing, but did you ever think that I might not know what I'm doing and saying it out loud helps me remember what I'm supposed to be doing?" I smiled back.

"God lord, why do I even talk to you?" She threw her hands up in the air.

We went through the building starting at the corner closest to Jefferson Street and the murder scene. Marcus, a black man in his late forties who'd worked for NYPD before taking early retirement, was covering the middle of the warehouse with quick, efficient sweeps of his flashlight. He'd actually taught me quite a bit about processing a scene. A lot of our guys didn't pay much attention to him, but once I figured out how much experience he'd gotten working in New York I started listening to him and asking questions. Knowing I'd pay attention to what he had to say, he'd throw me advice whenever he could.

Marcus and I were almost halfway done when Shantel yelled out, "Got something!"

She was standing near an old loading bay. As Marcus and I drew closer we could see she was standing on one side of the bay door. There were some pipes running down the wall nearby. She was shining her light at a spot on the floor.

"A drain and a faucet," Shantel said proudly. "Bet he chopped that man's fingers off and smashed his face right here."

I walked over to the wall and inspected the faucet. There was a little drop of moisture at the lip.

"Don't touch that. There might be some evidence there." Shantel couldn't resist being a smartass and getting back at me for earlier.

"Don't you know this is the sheriff's son? Investigatin' is in his blood," Marcus said, joining Shantel in ribbing me.

I pointed my flashlight at him. "Don't you start, or I'll have you standing in a cold warehouse collecting evidence all night. Oh wait, I'm going to do that anyway."

"Yay," Shantel said with false cheer.

"It's going to be a bitch finding out where the trap is for that drain." Marcus was getting serious about the job ahead of them.

"I'll go get some crime scene tape," Shantel said, turning and heading back toward their van.

I looked at my watch. It was close to two-thirty now. "We could use a couple more guys to help search the rest of the building, but we can wait until morning." I said. "I'm going up to the jail for a bit, then I'll be back."

I'd remembered Sykes telling me that they'd picked up Eddie Thompson. I might as well go talk to him. If he didn't have anything to do with this, then he could be released. Honestly, I didn't care why he'd run from me if it wasn't connected to this murder.

The jail was a separate building across the street from the sheriff's office. Not big, but it could house about thirty prisoners in a pinch. If we got more than thirty we had to start farming them out. I went in the front and put my Glock 17 pistol and magazines in a locker.

The deputies on duty at the jail always looked forlorn to

me. They were assigned to the jail for various reasons. Some of them were on light duty because of injuries or illness, while others were young officers being rotated through all the different possible duties of a deputy. I'd spent six months there and hated every day of it. Dealing with all the drunks, addicts and badass wannabes got old real quick. Out on the street you used the jail as the place you dumped the creeps when you were tired of dealing with them. Crap rolls downhill and the jail was the bottom of a mountain.

I was waiting in the interview room when they brought Eddie in. A tall man in his late twenties, he sat down in the chair across from me. Since I'd only requested that he be brought in for questioning, he wasn't handcuffed and they'd been keeping him in a comparatively comfortable private holding cell. His running had been a weak probable cause to bring him in, but luckily he hadn't lawyered up.

"I know who you are," he said. The guard who brought him in left and closed the door.

"Good for you. I know who you are too. Guess we're two well-informed people." I took out my notepad and set it on the table.

"Don't they record all of this?" he asked. His hair was long and black, contrasting oddly with his blue eyes. I could see the Thompson in him. He had the long face and Roman nose of the family patriarch, Daniel Thompson, who had been Calhoun's fire chief for many years until he retired.

"I'm not recording this interview."

He narrowed his eyes and his brow furrowed as he tried to decide if he could trust me or not.

"Why did you run when I came to AmMex on Tuesday?"

"I was wearing black lace underwear and thought you might arrest me."

For a minute I wasn't sure I'd heard him right. And then I was sure that I hadn't. "What?"

"You heard me," he said quietly, not quite meeting my eyes.

"What did you think I might arrest you for?"

"Who the hell knows? But that's what you all do."

"I don't have time for this bullshit." I decided to leave the lace panties alone.

"Okay, yeah, I could think of one or two things that you might have on me, but it's mostly stupid shit. Now I know why you were there. That body they found."

"Do you know anything about it?" I leaned in closer.

He raised his hands. "Nothing. I didn't see anything. And I don't know anything. Friend of mine from the trucking company I talked to after I ran said you'd found some body in a ditch not far from AmMex. That's it. Swear." He shrugged.

"But you ran anyway?"

This time he leaned forward. His voice was almost a whisper. "I told you, I was wearing panties."

Back to the panties. "What the hell?"

"I'm a cross-dresser. I like wearing lacy black panties. Now you can understand, I couldn't take a chance you might arrest me and bring me to jail. Things might not go so well if other people found out."

"Are you shitting me?" I watched his eyes, but he seemed to be dead serious.

"No, in fact, that's the other thing I wanted to talk to you about." Now he was whispering. "I need you to swear we aren't being recorded."

I had no idea where this was going. I pulled out my phone and showed him the recording app, currently not running. "If I got in here and felt like I needed to record a statement, I'd use this. But I'm not now."

He reached for my pad and pen. He looked me in the eyes one more time, then wrote on the pad, passing it to me when he was done. The note said: *I got information on some bad cops.*

"Here?" My voice was deadly serious.

His fingers were tapping nervously on the table and there was fear in his eyes. "Yeah, and in town too." He said the words fast, as though he wanted to get them out of his mouth and gone as quickly as possible.

I leaned back. I needed to think about this. The last thing a law enforcement officer wants to hear is that his department has corrupt officers in it. My dad being the sheriff made it twice as bad. I didn't want anything to do with it, but I didn't have a choice.

"Nothing is being recorded… that I know of."

He caught my drift right away. I really didn't think we were being recorded, but how the hell could I be sure? I didn't really believe there were any corrupt deputies; well, none that would do more than fudge their overtime slips, but here was an informant telling me that he had information.

I wrote *I'll pick you up in one hour at Jefferson and Park* on the pad and showed it to him. Eddie nodded. I got up and escorted him to the front desk, telling the sergeant at the desk that Eddie was free to go. The door buzzed and Eddie left while I went to retrieve my gun and mull over what he'd said and hadn't said.

CHAPTER SIX

I drove back to the murder scene, but in all honesty my mind wasn't on the case. Why the hell did this corrupt cop thing have to fall into my lap? I was wondering. I don't even like this job that much. Good thing, because if this goes anywhere I'll probably be out of the department. Hell, I might be in the witness protection program. Bad cops are bad news.

Pulling up at the warehouse, I found the evidence collection well underway. Pictures were being taken and everything was being examined and marked as evidence or not.

Shantel walked over to me. "This is a big pile of work you walked into."

"Tell me about it."

"I'm going to. The state boys are going to do most of the heavy lifting. We found some stains, most likely blood. We've swabbed it. Got someone trying to find the owner of the warehouse through the property records. He lives in Ohio or some such."

"Great," I said, not looking forward to dealing with an absentee owner and not paying much attention to Shantel. The corner of Park and Jefferson was about five minutes from the warehouse so I had some time before I needed to go meet with Eddie. I was half hoping he wouldn't show up.

"No sign of them fingers yet." She could tell my mind was on other things. "Am I boring you?" she asked, only half joking.

"No, just trying to see what it all means," I lied. The murder had slipped to second place in my priorities. "Who's here from the state?"

"You got lucky. They sent Trey." Shantel went back to where Marcus was using a screwdriver to take the cover off the drain.

I left the dismemberment site and walked out front to the murder scene. Trey Wilson finished talking to a photographer, patted him on the shoulder and came over to me.

"It's been here two days and you couldn't wait until the morning to call us?" He stuck out his hand good-naturedly. "How's your dad doing?" Trey was almost the same age as my dad, and had worked on a couple of important cases with him.

"He's doing great."

Trey was always a professional and was quick to move from the pleasantries into the nitty-gritty of the crime scene. "We've got a fairly confined area for the murder. This macadam makes it hard to pick up any tire tracks, but, on the good news side, if you can find the vehicle sooner rather than later, we might find some of the macadam stuck in the tire treads. Did you say the slug went through the body?"

"Yes, probably a twelve- or twenty-gauge."

"Where did your witness place the victim and the shooter?"

"He said the victim was on this side and the shooter close on that side."

"It's going to be a challenge finding the slug and, being a shotgun, it's not going to tell you too much without any rifling. But it would identify the gauge and possibly the make of the shell. Plus, when you find the perp you might find unfired shotgun shells that you can match it with. Can you give us some deputies to help search?"

"No problem. I'll get some guys together in the morning."

We went over a few more details before I glanced at my watch and saw that it was time to go meet my new best pain in the neck.

It was almost four-thirty when I drove through the intersection of Park and Jefferson the first time. I'd chosen it because it was tree-lined, so someone could wait in the shadows and not be seen. I didn't see him. It could mean that he was waiting in the shadows, hadn't gotten there yet or, if I was lucky, he wasn't going to show and I could forget he ever said anything.

Third time around the block and I saw him sitting in an older pickup truck about halfway down the block. I pulled in front of him, my unmarked car not likely to garner any unwanted attention. I unlocked the doors. Eddie quickly got out of his truck, hurried to my passenger side and got in the car.

"Shit, man." From the way he said it I could tell he'd taken a hit of something. Great, I thought, just great.

"Okay, what the hell do you know about crooked cops?" I was tired and really didn't want to be doing this.

"No. I want to work something out."

"What are you talking about? We didn't arrest you so there isn't anything to work out."

"This is about more than the cops."

I had known this was going to be complicated from the get-go. "Look, you got me here with the bad cops thing. That's what I need to hear about."

"I can give you a lot more than a few cops. You said you knew who I was, right?"

"Sure, you're Eddie Thompson, a petty crook."

"I'm not really a crook. I don't steal stuff." He actually

sounded offended.

I thought back over the offenses on his record. "Okay, fair enough, you have a couple of possessions, an assault and one or two other misdemeanors. Let's just admit you aren't one of the pillars of this community."

"But I'm a Thompson. My dad is Justin Thompson. My granddad is Daniel Thompson."

"Yeah, I can see the resemblance," I said sincerely.

"Fuck you too." The words were spit out with a harsh and bitter emotion.

"No love lost for your family, I see."

"That's why I want to work with you."

"What?" This was getting more confusing, not less.

"I know a lot of things about my family."

I remembered the Thompsons that worked in law enforcement and felt like I was beginning to see where this might be headed. "Like the Danny who works for our department?"

"Danny is okay. I'm talking about others, and not just my family. And it's not just the cops thing. In fact, I don't want to tell you that yet."

"Look, I don't have time for a bunch of bullshit."

"You really are bad at this, aren't you?"

What the hell? "What are you talking about?"

"I've heard them say that you don't want to be a deputy. You just sleepwalk through the job. You solve cases, but you don't really care."

"Look…" I really didn't know how to respond since it was pretty much the truth.

"See, I hear things. I can be your… informant."

"I still don't see your motivation."

"I told you. I'm a cross-dresser." He turned and looked out the window. "I didn't know what I was doing when I started dressing up. It just felt right. The day my dad caught me wearing my sister's panties and bra, he beat me so bad I couldn't go to school for a week. Mom and Dad told everyone I had the flu. I was eleven. I got caught again when

42

I was thirteen taking a pair of my cousin's Hello Kitty socks, and they found my stash of girl's clothes. Dad didn't beat me as bad, but he never let up after that. Cruel jokes at my expense. There was rough-housing where he'd encourage bigger boys to beat me up, put lipstick on me, all kinds of sadistic shit." His voice trailed off and he kept looking out the window.

I had gone from being annoyed to feeling quite a bit of sympathy for what he had to go through. Growing up with my dad had never been easy, but I'd always known that he loved me and would never purposefully hurt me. Eddie was clearly scarred by his experiences, but there was a strength to his words and emotions that proved he had not been drowned by the cruelty.

"I'll help you, but you're going to help me," he said, turning to look me in the face. I realized then that this might be the beginning of, not a friendship, but possibly some sort of strange partnership. "I'm saving the cops. If I gave you their names and what I know about them now, it wouldn't do you any good because I don't have any evidence."

"We can get the evidence if we know what we're looking for and who we're looking at."

"No way. If you act on what I know now, they'll be able to work it back and figure out it was me that told you. Other stuff first, and the cops later."

I thought about this. Pushing him too hard now might be a mistake. But it was going to be a bitch knowing that there were possibly corrupt deputies in our department and cops in town and not knowing who they were. But what choice did I have?

"Okay, we can play it your way for a while. But why me?"

"I figured you didn't care enough to beat the information out of me."

"I'll take that as a compliment. I've got two cases I need information on. First is the murder. Happened at the warehouse where the tracks cross Jefferson. Second is a fire in the Deep Water area."

"I'll get you something."

"If I don't hear from you pretty soon, I'm going to come back wanting to know a lot more about those cops. Understand?"

He looked at me and smiled. "You aren't very good at the tough guy routine."

"Screw you. Don't push it."

He nodded and got out of the car.

Back at the crime scene, Pete had arrived and was looking over the warehouse. He helped me organize half a dozen deputies and we scoured the area for the shotgun slug. Even using the height of the wound on the victim and the almost-level path of the bullet through his chest, without knowing exactly where he was standing and what angle he was facing it was a long shot. No luck. I called it off after four hours.

I was in the office before noon and got on the phone to New Orleans.

"Oh, right, I heard you called. Got the email." Dahlia sounded more upbeat and eager than I had imagined. I'd pictured a tattooed Goth girl in a permanent mope.

"Did you recognize the tattoo?"

"That's my work. And, oh yeah, I remember. Guy was pretty nice, but super particular about the needles and hygiene and everything. Not that I blame him. Just seemed a bit anal. Guess that's funny since I was tattooing his ass. So he's, like, dead?"

"Murdered."

"Really? Wow. Who would have thought that?"

"We're trying to figure out who he is. When did you do the tattoo?"

"A couple years ago. On… let's see… August second."

"You keep a record?"

"Well, I take a picture and there's a date on it. You got to have a book of your art. That way people can see if they want you to ink them or not. Lots of different artists, lots of different styles."

"But you didn't write down his name or anything?"

"No, it's about the art, not the person."

"But you talked to him, right?"

"Sure, it took hours to do this. Pretty complex design."

"Did he live in New Orleans? Or close by?"

"Noooo, I don't think so. We get some local business, but we're pretty close to the Quarter and most of it's tourists. Like I said, he seemed very concerned that we follow all the health regulations. This was his first tattoo."

"And his last. You don't remember his name? Or anything else?"

"I'm rotten with names. Show me a piece of art, and I'll remember where and when I saw it, but a name, nah. Hey, wait, he did talk about his job, I think. Something funny... I wasn't too interested, but I thought it odd that he did it."

"Anything might help. Was it odd because he did the job or was the job itself odd?"

"Ohhhh, I'm thinking. Oh, yeah, he like, sold stuff to hospitals. Like beds and machines and stuff. Just seemed funny."

Something else occurred to me. I've been to New Orleans a number of times, and with that tattoo... "Was he gay?"

"Well, I don't know. I don't think he was very effeminate, but sexual preference didn't really come up."

I could tell the question irritated her a little. "I'm just trying to find out who he was and what happened to him."

"It was August. I'd have to look, but I think it was before Southern Decadence."

"Southern Decadence?"

"The big gay pride thing here in New Orleans. Takes place every August. I think it was later than the second. If it was during the event, well then, most of our customers who come in are there for the event."

I figured I'd milked this for everything I was going to get. So I asked her to send me a copy of her picture for the record and got some other contact information from her.

I went back to the crime scene after the call. Everything had pretty much been done except for taking the drain completely apart. I'd finally gotten in touch with the owner and brought him up to date. I'd asked him for permission to take the drain apart. He was very cooperative and told me to do whatever I needed to do. Usually with a business property, the first question you get is "Are you going to pay to put it back together?" anytime you have to start dismantling stuff. But there really are nice guys who just want to help. I made up my mind that we would do a good job putting everything back together and leave the place better than we found it.

CHAPTER SEVEN

I was just thinking about a late lunch when I got a text from Dad: *Meet me at the hospital in Tallahassee.* Why would you send that to a family member without elaborating? A couple more messages back and forth told me that he just wanted me to be there when he went to visit an old friend. This all made sense. Dad hated hospitals more than most people. I wasn't real fond of them for the same reason. We'd spent a wretched month at the hospital as my mother was dying.

I found him leaning against his car in the parking lot. It was a beautiful sunny day with a cool fall wind out of the north.

"I hate hospitals," he stated as I walked up. "You know, I cannot forget the odor of the place when your mother was lying there with tubes running in her arms and down her throat. And the worthless doctors telling me there was nothing that could be done." Anger lived in every word.

I patted him on the shoulder.

"Anyway, thanks for coming. I need to see Jim. From what I've heard he's not going to know I'm there, but..."

Jim Devries was one of the largest land-owners in the county and came from one of the first families to settle there back in the 1830s. He was also an old friend of Dad's.

They'd grown up together. Jim had had a stroke about a week ago, followed closely by a heart attack. He couldn't breathe on his own and the stroke had left him incoherent.

Coming off the elevator on the third floor, we turned right and headed to the ICU. Little had changed from a decade earlier when I ran down the hall to find my father crying and pounding on the wall with his fist. My mother had had an aneurysm and was in a coma by the time they moved her up to the ICU. Sudden, unexpected, tragic—all the words mean nothing when you're left reeling in pain and anger. It was almost a month before the machines were turned off and my mother went back to Adams County to rest beneath a sycamore tree in Abagail Cemetery.

In the small family area outside of the ICU we met Tim, Jim's son. A few years older than me, he was stocky and round-faced. There was just a touch of premature grey around his temples. He smiled when he saw us and came over, giving Dad a hardy handshake and a manly hug.

"Thanks for coming," Tim said. "I think a lot of folks have already put him in his grave."

"I understand how you feel." I knew Dad meant that too. "He's a good man. A strong man."

"I keep hoping something will change. It was so damn sudden."

"What do the doctors say?"

"They aren't giving him much chance of recovery. Yesterday one of them told me he wouldn't be able to survive without the ventilator and that he'd suffered severe brain damage." His voice was numb with grief. "You can go see him."

Dad nodded and we went up to the desk to be admitted to the unit. Jim looked horrible. A strong man who'd worked his farm every day of his life, and two weeks ago could have crushed my hand with his, lay on the bed looking like a breathing corpse. Dad held his hand and told him we were there. He stared down at his childhood friend, seeing the past and the terrifying future that we all face. Finally, he gently laid Jim's hand down and turned away. I followed him back out of the ICU.

Tim was talking to a younger woman. I remembered there was a daughter.

"Sheriff, you remember my sister, Tilly." Tim spoke with no emotion. The air felt tense.

"Of course, but you were smaller the last time I saw you," Dad said to Tilly.

"It has been a few years." She smiled.

"How's your mother?"

"Same, hell on wheels. She won't come by and see Daddy."

"Why should she? She damn near broke him when she left." Tim wasn't even trying to hide his anger. "I'm not sure why *you* came back. Oh, yeah, I think I know."

"Tim, I don't think we need to air our dirty laundry in front of friends." Her voice dripped with venom masquerading as honey.

"For once you're right." Tim turned to us. "I do appreciate you coming by, and I know it would mean a lot to Dad." We shook hands with Tim and shared awkward hugs with Tilly.

"She takes after her mother, all right," Dad said, pressing the lobby button in the elevator. "Margret was a queen bitch. Loved Jim's money, but him, not so much."

"When did she leave him?"

"It was as much him kicking her out as her leaving. About ten or twelve years ago. I think Tilly was fourteen, maybe younger, at the time... something like that. Went with her mother. Jim gave her a nice settlement. He didn't like lawyers and hated the idea of going to court so he pretty much gave her what she wanted. She moved over to Jacksonville or someplace, which suited Jim. But he was heartbroken when Tilly went with her mom. Of course she was a teenager and who can figure them out? Her mom offered her the city and shopping sprees while Jim only knew about farming and hard work."

We were out by the cars when Dad turned to me. "I need to get back to the office. Would you go by the house and pick up Mauser? He's got a vet appointment."

I was just able to choke back the *What the hell?* that came to mind. "Okay," I heard myself saying, fighting back my annoyance.

I picked Mauser up at Dad's house. The sitter handed me Mauser's travel bags—yes, two reusable grocery bags full of treats, water bottles, poopy bags and toys for a ten-mile trip to the vet.

Of course Dad had failed to make going to the vet fun for Mauser, so as soon as we pulled into the parking lot he set his paws in the carpet of the van and his eyes got a determined look. Treats had no effect on him if he didn't want to do something. A couple of Scooby Snacks weren't going to get him out of the van and into the vet. All hundred and ninety pounds were planted firmly inside the vehicle and no amount of tugging on his harness was going to work.

I glanced at my watch and saw that we were already five minutes late for his appointment. I closed the van doors and headed in to tell the receptionist that we were there, but we just weren't *there*.

I had just turned from the front desk when a woman came out of the back.

"Is that Mauser in the van?" Obviously a rhetorical question since the van had Dad's election signs all over it and a giant dog head looking around defiantly from the back. But I answered anyway.

"Yes, sorry, I'm trying to get him out. If Dad had worked a little harder at teaching him that going to the vet is fun, this would be a heck—" I noticed that the vet tech was following me outside "—of a lot easier."

"Mauser!" she called.

To my shock, he stood up and gave half a bark. I quickly clicked the van's remote and the door slid open. Mauser jumped out and bounded over to the small woman, affectionately bumping into her.

I took a long look at this pied piper of Great Danes. Her name tag said "Cara Laursen," and she looked to be a couple years younger than me. She was quite pretty, with dark red hair done up in a double braid, fair skin and petite features that fit her stature. *Good God, I'm as attracted to her as Mauser is.*

"Come on, boy, let's go in and let the doc take a look at you." Mauser and I followed her back into the office.

"Thanks a million," I said to her as I put Mauser's leash on him. "It might have taken me an hour to get him in here."

"Oh, he and I are old friends." She smiled and Mauser looked up at her adoringly. I just hoped my face didn't look as goofy as his.

Doctor Barnhill had heard the joke more than once that his name would be a better fit for a large animal vet. But he seemed fine with Mauser being his largest patient. He came in and wrestled with the beast, taking his temperature, a fecal sample and a blood sample. Mauser seemed to be willing to put up with all of it as long as he could see Cara. She would smile at him as she handed the doctor a syringe or whatever else he needed, and Mauser would keep his big dopey eyes glued to her every move.

"Do you have this effect on every dog?" I flirted with her. By the look the doctor gave me, I could tell she had the same effect on every four- *and* two-footed dog that came into the office.

"Guess it's my superpower," she said, turning the smile onto me for a moment. My mind was running through every possible scenario to get a date with her. Unfortunately for me, my mind didn't have too much experience getting dates with strangers. Suddenly we were done. Mauser got an "okay" from the doc and we were being ushered out of the exam room. I was losing my opportunity fast. The receptionist told me I could go and she'd just bill my dad.

We would be out the door in a minute with no good

excuse for coming back in to make a date. When I thought all was lost, Mauser earned my everlasting gratitude by turning and tugging his way back toward Cara, who was heading back into the examining rooms.

"Whoa, boy-o," I said half-heartedly as he pulled me back toward Cara. She turned and laughed at the sight of me being dragged across the tile floor toward her. I would have gladly been pulled across broken glass barefoot to hear her musical laugh. *She's a witch*, I thought. *She's put a spell on me.* I'd never fallen for someone that fast. Never.

"Maybe you could walk us out," I said. *Clever boy*, I mentally congratulated myself.

"Sure, no problem. You good with that, Mauser?"

He leaned into her, ignoring me at the other end of his leash. We all walked back out to the van where I opened the cargo door and Mauser reluctantly hopped in. I quickly shut the door.

"You all take care," Cara smiled, turning back toward the office.

"Wait." *Okay, smart guy, now what?*

She turned back, looking at me. I was frozen.

"Yes?"

"Umm, should I have scheduled another appointment for him?" Dumbest question ever.

"No. We'll send your dad a postcard when Mauser's due for his next checkup." She stood still, facing me. She must have known that I wanted to ask something else.

"I... Would you like to have lunch sometime?" I blurted out like a puberty-challenged teenager.

"Well... Maybe." *Maybe?* That felt like a punch in the gut.

"Oh, I'm sorry. Are you seeing someone?" Like it was any of my business.

"Sort of. Nothing too serious, but life's a little complicated right now." There was my answer—a pretty clear "go away and quit bothering me."

"No problem. Take care." I beat a hasty retreat to the driver's side of the van. She turned and walked back inside.

When I got in the driver's seat I looked back at Mauser, who gave me a disgusted look and burped deeply into my face. "For once, you're right, I'm an idiot." I started the engine and took Mauser home.

Pete was waiting for me when I finally got back to the office.

"We finished up at the crime scene. They got some good stuff out of the drain. Said we should get a DNA match with our victim in a week. I've gone through most of the hotels and motels in the area. So far no one has a guest that's disappeared or failed to check out. I'll keep on it. I interviewed a dozen people who lived in the neighborhood close to the warehouse. Got nothing. Not too surprising since all of the houses are at least a quarter mile away. Also, gun shots aren't that unusual south of the tracks. But I'll check back on the ones who weren't home."

Pete rattled all of this off quickly and efficiently. He was effective when he was present, awake and not eating or reading anything.

"Thanks, Pete. You got any cases we should be working on?" I knew he'd taken a couple of calls while I'd been out doing personal chores for Dad.

"A possible car-jacking, but I think he's bullshitting me. My guess, he traded it for drugs and the report is for the insurance and his wife. I'll lean on him when wifey isn't hanging over his shoulder. We also got a heads-up from the Tallahassee police. They had to handle a public disturbance call at the hospital. You won't believe this one. Tim and Tilly Devries."

He had my full attention. "Richest family in the county, and the brother and sister are shoving and slapping each other at the hospital." He was shaking his head in wonder.

"I'll take that and look into it." I wasn't sure exactly why I wanted to get involved. Maybe because their father was a good friend of Dad's? I didn't know, but I felt that this was something I should deal with. Pete, as usual, had no problem passing work on to someone else.

"Works for me. I talked to the TPD officer who responded. He said it was all over by the time he got there, but that they both had marks on them. The hospital wouldn't drop it either. Corporate policy or some crap."

"I'll talk to all the parties and come up with some kind of resolution. Not much to worry about anyway. The State Attorney isn't going to file any complaints against the Devrieses unless there is blood on the ground. Even then it would have to be a lot of blood."

"Must be nice to have money. Shouldn't say that, I guess... Tim and Jim are two of the most upright people in this county. Bet you they haven't missed a church service in years. And they take all that Jesus stuff to heart." Pete's wife was always nagging him about going to church instead of spending his Sundays puttering around his garage or at the gun range.

But Pete was right about the Devrieses. Some of the large landowners were mean in every sense of the word, but the Devries family contributed to almost any charity in the county that was worthy. And I'd never heard anyone say a bad word about any of them.

"Mrs. Devries, now that's a different story. She spent money on herself and the kids and to hell with everyone else. Has a tongue that could cut steel. Just the opposite of Jim and Tim. Don't think I ever heard anyone say a good word about her. Maybe the daughter got a little bit of the pit viper in her." Pete looked at his watch. "I'm gonna head out for the day."

"See you tomorrow," I said to his back, and he waved over his shoulder in acknowledgement. I went over to his desk and rooted around until I found the report from Tallahassee on the Devrieses little altercation. I skimmed the narrative.

Complainant, Mrs. Blackman, R.N., stated that when she heard raised voices she looked over and Tilly Devries shoved her brother, Tim Devries, who in turn shoved his sister. She then slapped him across the face, at which point he shouted "Bitch" in a very loud voice and slugged or slapped his sister back. At this point Dr. Chandler tried to intervene and slipped and fell on the floor. A male nurse, Bob Lansky, rushed over and grabbed Tim, which allowed the sister to scratch Tim's face. Dr. Chandler had gotten back to his feet by now and pulled Tilly away from Tim. Security showed up in a couple of minutes and both parties were told they would have to wait for the police to arrive since they had already been called. When I arrived I talked to both parties and got them to write up a statement (attachment A and B). Per the request of the hospital, I told each of them that they would need to leave the premises and to contact the administration before they could return. They agreed. Tim's injuries were treated before he left the hospital.

Typical report. I picked up the phone and called Tim after finding his number in the report.

"Tim, this is Deputy Larry Macklin."

"I really appreciate you and your dad coming by the hospital."

"I was glad that I had the chance to see you father. But there seems to have been some trouble between you and your sister after we left."

"Nothing, really. She can be so damn cold. Wants me to take Dad off the respirator."

"It's hard, but families sometimes have to make these hard decisions. But throwing punches in a hospital is not the way to do it," I said in my stern deputy voice.

"I know, I know. She just gets to me. Look, can you talk to the hospital? I need to get back there and be with my dad." There was grief and something else in his voice. Regret? Still some anger?

"I'm not going to do that until I'm satisfied that you all aren't going to get into another altercation. Someone could get hurt, like the doctor who ended up on the floor during y'all's little boxing match."

"I'm not going to cause any trouble. My sister's the one who needs to keep her distance." There it was... definitely anger.

"I'll talk to her too."

"She shoved me first!" Okay, we were back on the playground.

"Tim, this is not the time to be feuding with your sister. Your father needs both of you to come together. I suggest that you all don't talk about removing the ventilator unless there is a doctor or someone else from the hospital there to help explain the medical and legal issues to you both. My father and I had to go through this when my mother was dying. I know it's difficult. Sometimes there just doesn't seem to be a right answer. Now, if you can promise me that you will avoid talking to Tilly about any… uh… emotional subjects unless there is a third party present to keep the tempers in check, I'll talk to Tilly and then the hospital and get your visiting privileges restored."

"Of course." He sounded more subdued. "I appreciate you taking this on. You can count on me. Good luck with Tilly."

He seemed to have let some of the anger and frustration go. I remembered what Pete had said about father and son attending church.

"Tim, why don't you talk with your minister too."

"Actually, I just got off the phone with him. You don't have to worry about me. But thanks."

We said our goodbyes and I reluctantly called Tilly. She screamed at me for five minutes, swearing that she loved her father more than Tim ever did and that she should be the one to take care of their father. I didn't ask her what she meant by "take care of." Eventually, she wound down and I was able to elicit the same promises from her that I got from her brother.

A call to the hospital got them to agree not to pursue the issue, but the case would stay open so that if anything else happened there was a record showing that the hospital had been on top of it. Typical CYA. Tim and Tilly were told that their visiting privileges were reinstated, leaving me done for the day. Exhausted from almost two days without sleep, I headed home.

CHAPTER EIGHT

Friday I was up and at my desk early. I wanted to see if I could make any headway with the single clue I had on my John Doe, that he sold stuff to hospitals. It was a daunting prospect, knowing just how much stuff a hospital must buy every week, let alone in a month or a year.

I powered up my computer and went straight to my email. One message jumped out. It was from Dahlia and said:

You aren't too good at this job, are you? LOL. You didn't think to ask me if I could remember his face. I'm an artist. I'm much more likely to remember what something looks like than to remember its name. This goes for people too. Attached is a drawing based on what I remembered.

I opened up the picture and saw a middle-aged man looking back at me. Naturally, I couldn't tell if it was a good likeness, but it certainly was a fine drawing. The forensic artist had confirmed Dr. Darzi's prediction that it was going to take a while to do a facial reconstruction from the badly damaged face. Since the bones had been smashed, it would have to be stripped of flesh and the bones put back together before they could do a full reconstruction and rendering. Having Dahlia's drawing at least gave me something to work with until then. Dahlia was definitely on my Christmas list.

I could now send the picture to hospitals and ask if this man sold them equipment or supplies. Much better than asking if they knew a salesman with "Kiss My Ass" tattooed on his butt.

I started the grunt work, which involved much less grunting than in the old days thanks to the Internet. I built a list of hospitals in the southeast, got contact emails for them and began sending out my request for information.

It was past noon by the time I was done. Pete had come and gone. He hadn't had any luck with witnesses around the warehouse. We were just damn lucky we had the witness that we did.

I ate lunch at the Donut Hole. I know, cops and donuts—ha, ha. But they actually made great croissant sandwiches. While I chewed I wondered if I'd ever hear from Eddie Thompson, my new confidential informant. If it was a big dodge, he'd done too good a job of salting the mine. I wanted to know more about the dirty cops. Particularly any dirty deputies. It wasn't as much for me as it was for Dad. Whatever came out of the department was his responsibility. Having a scandal happen while he was sheriff would be like getting stabbed in the heart. I'd give Eddie a couple more days before I went looking for him.

I checked my email on my phone. Why is it when you send something out you feel like you should get an instant reply? I'd sent over a hundred emails to more than fifty hospitals. Two to each, covering both their security offices and whatever department looked like it handled procurement.

Score! There were three replies. Even though they just acknowledged the receipt of the email and assured me they would make inquiries, it still made me feel better getting something back.

I swung by the murder scene one more time, just so I could

walk it without being distracted by the techs and deputies. I asked myself why the killer had chosen this spot.

The warehouse sat on the edge of town, near the railroad tracks that really separated the haves from the have-nots. The old saying about the wrong side of the tracks was still true in a lot of smaller towns in the South and Calhoun was no different. The warehouse would certainly have been deserted at that hour and any mess that was made wouldn't be noticed right away. Without the witness coming forward we still wouldn't know where the murder was committed.

Why chop off his fingers and bludgeon his face? Could it be something more than just trying to obscure his identity? The act of mutilation spoke of anger and passion. A lover? A family member?

Pete pulled into the warehouse.

"See anything you didn't see before?" he asked.

I nodded. "This was an arranged meeting. It's not like a bar parking lot where you might just bump into someone and get into a fight. Either the victim or the shooter arranged this meeting."

"See, you're getting the hang of this detective business."

I held up my middle finger.

"Do you remember what was here before the warehouse?" I asked for no good reason.

Pete thought about it for a while. "Nothing much. An old juke joint. Good place for it near the tracks. No houses around, but convenient to town."

"When was it torn down?"

"Well, it fell down, mostly. It closed and opened a couple of times. The last was about 1980. Was an eyesore for years. Kids still came out here and parked. Finally the city decided to make this an industrial park, got some federal funds and put in the warehouses."

I looked around, trying to imagine an old frame house in the woods full of rhythm and blues music and drunken partiers. History fascinated me and even fairly recent history could captivate my imagination.

"Think I'll head over to the library and see what they have about it."

"Better off going to see Albert Griffin."

"The Adams County Historical Society? Good idea. He work?"

"Retired two years ago."

"Leave your car here and we'll ride over together." This saved me having to get directions and having to introduce myself. I'd been to some of the society's talks, but I was only halfway to their sixty-year-old minimum age requirement. Okay, they didn't really have a minimum age, but seriously, their meetings looked like bingo night at the senior center.

"You really think you're going to learn anything about this crime from the historical society?"

"Now how the hell am I going to know if I don't go and talk to them?"

"You're just killing time," Pete said accusingly.

"Of course."

"Whatever. I'm in. Nothing waiting back at the big house but cases."

"Good man." And off we went.

Mr. Griffin was remarkably robust. He opened the door and ushered us into a room that looked like someone had turned the Library of Congress upside down and dumped all the books into his house. It was beautiful.

He cleared a couple chairs by moving books and shooing cats. One big black cat sniffed me, smelled Ivy and glared at me in disapproval before sauntering off. Pete and Mr. Griffin seemed to be old friends, or at least all of their relatives seemed to know each other and intermingle freely. There was about half an hour of "how's this person doing" and "when did you last see that person." Finally, Pete told him why we were there and the old man looked thoughtful.

"The Kettle. That's what it was called originally. First time I found it mentioned was in a court document. There had been an altercation between a couple of customers that resulted in a white man getting shot. This was, ummmm, let me see, 1897 or '98. Big brouhaha about shutting it down. A couple of weeks after the shooting there was an editorial in the paper and then letters decrying the depravity that went on there. End result was that a black man, Ezra or Ezariah or something like that, was tried for the crime. The community was very proud of the fact that they actually tried him and didn't take him immediately to the nearest live oak tree. And The Kettle was closed down for the first time. Stayed closed through the winter and reopened quietly in the late spring."

"Didn't stay closed?"

"I imagine most of the town fathers went there to get a little liquor and what-have-you, so those doors weren't going to remain locked. Pretty much established a pattern. Joint opened, trouble happened, town shocked to discover it existed, joint closed, then joint quietly reopend."

He dug through some books. "There are some pictures of it during the forties and fifties. That was the joint's glory days. By the way, that's what most people called it—just 'the joint.' Ah, here."

He handed me a large old photo album. It was open to a page that had about a dozen pictures taken at different times. One showed black soldiers in World War II uniforms, another was of a couple fifties-style convertibles with the tops down and overflowing with young people smiling and clowning it up for the camera. In all of the pictures was an old wooden house with a wraparound front porch, lights strung around it and old advertisements for cigarettes, chewing gum and Coke.

"What about more recently?" I asked.

"Honestly, it went downhill. Changed hands a lot in the sixties and seventies. Finally the world had moved beyond juke joints. Late seventies and eighties, high school kids went there to get in trouble, if you know what I mean."

He held up his hand and got a serious look on his face.

"I'm not making light of it either. I've taken a number of oral histories and, honestly, some really bad stuff happened out there. I know women were raped. I think we're lucky there weren't any murders out there then."

"We don't know there weren't," I said bluntly, thinking about predators like Ted Bundy or Son of Sam.

He gave me a thoughtful look. "I know your dad. He was in one of my classes when I taught at the high school. You remind me of him."

"I know when I'm being insulted," I laughed.

"No, really. He impressed me a great deal."

"We've wasted enough of your time." I stood up and Pete climbed up out of an old wingback chair. As Mr. Griffin escorted us back through the stacks of books and folders, I saw that black cat eyeing me with a look of good riddance on his face.

We each had four new cases on our desks. I sat down and called the victim on each, introduced myself and assured them that I would get back to them soon. An auto theft resolved itself. Turned out the wife had loaned it to a relative that the husband didn't approve of so the wife didn't tell the husband, etc., etc. I didn't need all the family history. I was happy to stamp "closed" on the folder and spend ten minutes closing it out on the computer.

After that I went through my emails. Damned if there wasn't a positive response from a hospital in Pensacola. I picked up the phone and called the contact on the email. It being Friday afternoon, I wasn't surprised to get voicemail. I banged out a reply to the email asking them to call or give me the best time to contact them.

Matt came in with two other deputies, looking particularly smug. He stopped at my desk and slapped a flyer on it. It announced that Calhoun's chief of police was running for sheriff.

"Guess your dad's going to have a little competition next

year."

That explained the smug look. Matt and the chief had been high school bros. Little did Matt know that I'd celebrate Dad losing the election. Hell, I might even vote for the other guy. I had my reasons for being a deputy, and they were complicated, but if Dad lost it would make it easier for me to quit and do something I really wanted to do. But unless the sun started rising in the west, the chief didn't stand a chance against Dad. But then I remembered Eddie and the potential for a scandal. While I might be fine with Dad losing in a straight-up contest, the thought of him being blindsided by a late-in-the-game scandal didn't sit well.

I picked up the flyer. "Will that make you first deputy if your bromance buddy becomes sheriff?" As one of the other deputies snickered at my joke, I saw blood in Matt's eyes.

CHAPTER NINE

I told Ivy all about Mr. Griffin's black cat and Matt over dinner. She seemed unimpressed with my daily challenges. Another Friday night at home. I almost wished I was on call so I had an excuse for not having a date.

Thinking of Cara, I asked Ivy, "How would you like to go to the vet?" and received only a cold stare. I started to think this was going to be a rough weekend.

My phone rang about nine o'clock.

"This is Brenda Hart from Pensacola Memorial Hospital. I got your email. I hope this isn't too late to call."

"No, not at all. Though I'm a little surprised. I didn't think I'd hear back from anyone until Monday."

"Ha! I can't remember the last time I went more than a couple of hours without checking my work email."

"Checking and getting back are two different things."

"True," she said, giving a little laugh. "I wanted to get back as soon as possible since it involved a murder. And, honestly, if it is Mark Kemper, well, he was always such a nice guy…" She trailed off.

"You said the picture I sent you looks like this guy Mark Kemper?" I eased Ivy off my lap and got a pen and paper to make notes.

"Yes. The resemblance is pretty good."

"And who is Mark Kemper?"

"He sells, well, just about anything to us. He represents a wholesale medical supply company out of Texas. Mark comes by every month, or sometimes more often, and shows us the latest and greatest while finding out what we need. As I said, he's really a nice guy who seems to live and breathe medical equipment. He can rattle off the specs on almost anything he sells."

"Do you have a number for him? Or some other way of reaching him?"

"I've already tried the phone number I have for him. I did that before sending you the email. I didn't want to bother you if I could just pick up the phone and call him and know he wasn't your victim."

"But he didn't answer."

"No, and I called Texas Health Supply and they couldn't reach him either."

"Did he live in Texas?"

She was quiet for a minute. "I don't think so. As much as he talked, he didn't talk much about himself. He was a very good salesman, always on topic. I've got the company's phone number."

"Please," I said and wrote the number down as she recited it. "Is there anything else you can think of that might help us?"

"No, I really can't."

"I appreciate you calling. If you think of anything else, give me a call."

"I will… And would you let me know if the… body is Mark. He was really well liked by a lot of our staff. We'd want to do something for his family." She added quickly, "I hope it isn't him."

"I'll let you know one way or the other."

I tried calling Kemper's company as soon as I hung up. It was after their business hours, so my options were to leave a message or call back. I elected to call back.

"Time for Google," I told Ivy, who was busy cleaning her paws. Searching for Mark Kemper gave me a zillion hits. I added medical supplies to the search field and clicked on images. My eyes were immediately drawn to Brenda Hart's Mark Kemper. He certainly did look a lot like Dahlia's picture. Strange… How did the "Kiss My Ass" tattoo fit with the description of Mark Kemper that Brenda gave me? Super nice guy gets a message like that inked on his butt? *Mark Kemper, if you are my corpse, I'm interested in learning more about you*, I thought

More Googling found his Facebook page, which told me Mark was gay. The relationship field was blank. There were several Kempers on his list of friends. After a moment or two of soul searching, I messaged three adult Kempers. I told all of them who I was and asked if they had recently had contact with Mark or knew where he had been during the last week. I added that we were concerned for his wellbeing and that they could contact me via Facebook or through the Adams County Sheriff's Office. My cell number was on my office voicemail.

Twenty minutes later my phone rang.

"Is this Larry Macklin?" a breathless voice asked.

"Yes, it is."

"I'm Mary Kemper. Mark is my son. Is he all right? Has there been an accident?" The fear in her voice was palpable over the phone.

"Mrs. Kemper, we don't know much at this point. We don't even know if your son is the person we need to find." I was trying not to alarm her in case it wasn't the body of her son in the morgue. "If you can answer a couple questions, that might help us to clear this whole thing up." I was trying to use my best "calm the person down" voice. "Can you do that?"

"Yes, of course."

"Do you know where your son is?"

"No, no, that's why I called when my sister-in-law said she'd received a message from you. I haven't heard from him in days and he never goes that long without calling me. Please, if you know where he is…"

I was having to think hard to come up with the right questions without letting her know the potential heartbreak she was facing. "Do you know if your son was in New Orleans a couple years ago?"

"What does that have to do with where he is now?" she pleaded.

"Please, if you could answer the questions, that would really help."

"Yes, he went to New Orleans. He travels a lot for business, but goes to New Orleans a lot when he's off too." She got real quiet than added, "His partner used to live there."

There was no way to shield her from the question I needed to ask, but I wanted to have some insurance if the answer was yes. "Mrs. Kemper, is anyone else with you?"

"My husband is… is in the other room. He and Mark don't get along. So I came in this room to call. Why?"

"Does your son have a tattoo?"

"Oh, my God, yes, he has a tattoo. What? Tell me, is he okay?"

I had no choice but to plow ahead. I was sorry I had started this tonight. "Is it on his… rear end?"

"Oh, God, yes. It says…" She was starting to cry now. "Kiss my ass." She laughed and began to cry. I could hear a man's voice in the background, asking what was wrong.

"I'm so sorry, Mrs. Kemper. We have a body in our morgue that matches your son's description."

Crying and wailing came from the other end of the phone. Mr. Kemper picked up the phone and I explained everything to him. His voice was cold and emotionless… or maybe he was just as devastated as his wife. It's hard to judge a person's reaction over the phone. He told me that they lived in Texas, but would make arrangements to come to Tallahassee to identify their son's body.

And then he said something that took me by surprise. He

said they didn't need directions. They had lived in Adams County for almost twenty years. Then he hung up, leaving me to ponder the connection that brought Mark Kemper home to Adams County to be shot.

I spent another hour tracking down the hotel where Mark had stayed, finally finding it in Tallahassee. We'd called the hotel earlier in our search for a guest that hadn't checked out, but since he'd used his credit card and left his check-out date open, the hotel was still happily charging his card. They didn't care if anyone was coming or going from the room or not. I told them not to let anyone else go in or out of the room, then I called the Tallahassee police and asked if one of their officers could go by and put crime scene tape across the door. I'd go over there with some of our techs in the morning.

The next day I drove to Tallahassee and met Shantel and Marcus, who frequently tried to schedule their shifts together. Kemper's room was neat and orderly. Unfortunately, it was clear that the maids had cleaned the room since the last time he'd been there. The two things I'd hoped to find, a laptop or his phone, were not there. He'd probably had his phone with him, but I had thought there was some chance that a laptop might have been left behind. Maybe if we found his car. But the killer had had access to the car, so that would probably be a dead end... No pun intended.

We went over everything else in the room, but found nothing unusual or that would give us any new leads. Marcus and Shantel did the full fiber-and-hair-collection routine on the off chance that the perpetrator had come to Mark's room at some point. It wouldn't help us find the killer, but the evidence might help to convict him.

On my way home I drove by the arson site to have a look at it in daylight. It was still a mess and didn't look like anyone had done anything with it.

On Sunday I got a call from Eddie which, needless to say, surprised me. He said he'd been trying to find information on the arson or the murder. One of his cousins did say a friend of a friend had been talking about arson and how to do it. He swore he'd try to learn more. I almost believed him.

Monday was rainy and cold. The Halloween decorations had almost all disappeared and Thanksgiving was only two weeks away. As I worked on my back log of cases, Mr. Kemper called and said they would be at my office by noon. I told him to meet me at the hospital in Tallahassee instead. I felt like every word I spoke drove home his new reality of a world without a son.

According to my weather app, the front was stalled on top of us so we'd have rain for the next day or two. When I drove into the hospital parking lot, I saw the Kempers standing by what I assumed was their rental car. The sky mirrored the grief on the Kempers' faces. They both appeared to be in their seventies and in good health, but it was obvious that the ordeal had Mrs. Kemper near to an emotional collapse.

"Both of you don't have to go in," I told them, trying hard to dissuade Mrs. Kemper from the ordeal. "His face was badly damaged. We're going to keep that covered unless you feel that you need to see it in order to make an identification." I was grateful for small favors that we had found his folks before forensics removed his head in order to do a facial reconstruction.

Mr. Kemper handed me an envelope. "His dental records. He had good teeth," he said flatly. Mrs. Kemper stood slightly back from her husband. He glanced at her. "It's up to you if you go in." His voice held no gentleness. It was pretty clear that this marriage had been dead for a long time.

"I want to see him. Why *you're* here, I don't know. You told him you never wanted to see him again." My heart was breaking for her. At this point I was just hoping that this toxic relationship didn't explode into violence.

"It's my duty." He spat the words at her. Kemper turned to me. "Let's get this over with." Now he was echoing my sentiments.

I had called ahead and given the morgue assistant very detailed instructions on how to present the body. Tattoo first with as much of the body's ass covered as possible. Close the curtains, roll the body over and, with the face and genitalia covered, open the curtains again. Just to be clear, I told the fellow I spoke with that if he caused the family any more grief or indignity than necessary, I would be forced to make sure that he never drove anywhere again without a law enforcement officer pulling him over and giving him a ticket.

Thank God the Kempers were able to identify him without looking at his face. The huge "Y" incision in his chest plus the large wound caused by the shotgun slug were bad enough.

I got permission to use one of the rooms in the hospital's security office to interview the Kempers. With the animosity between the two of them, I wanted to interview them separately. I took Mrs. Kemper first.

Mrs. Kemper sat down at the table and I took the chair across from her. I almost wanted to reach out and take her hand, but she kept them back. Her right hand clenched and unclenched around a Kleenex.

"I can't imagine how difficult this must be for you. Let me start by saying how sorry I am, and I assure you that I will do everything I can to find the person who did this. We have a witness and some physical evidence." Not too damn much evidence, but I wouldn't tell her that.

"This is a nightmare," she whispered.

There was nothing I could do for her so I pushed on. "I need to ask you some questions. The more information I have, the easier it will be for me to find the monster who killed your son." Seeing the pain that this old woman was suffering made me all the more determined to solve this case. This was a premeditated murder and it had devastated more than one life.

"I loved my son," Mrs. Kemper said emphatically, as though there could be any question. "You know, I was shocked when he first told me. It took me some time to understand that him being that way wasn't the end of the world. I loved him. My boy." Her eyes were unfocused as she talked. If her husband wouldn't serve as a sounding board for her grief, it was the least that I could do.

She went on. "That man, his father…" The words were spat out. "I tried to make him understand, to see it the way I saw it. But he refused to see him."

"Why?"

"My son was gay." She looked up and met my eyes as though she expected me to shame her for loving him.

"There's no shame in that."

"I know that," she snapped at me before her eyes softened. "Where we lived, the times we grew up in… I wasn't sure at first. But he was my son. That didn't make a difference to *him*… Did this… have something to do with him being gay?"

"I don't know."

"You hear about gay men being beat up… even killed."

"It's one of the possibilities that we'll look into. Where was your son living?"

"Alabama, Mobile. He sold things to hospitals. Mobile was about in the middle of the area he traveled."

I'd need his address and might have to go search his house, but that could wait. "Did he have a… boyfriend?"

"They broke up two years ago. They'd been together for so long. Very painful for Mark."

"Why did they break up?"

"Tony, Tony Frye, that's his name. He wanted to live somewhere else. He told Mark that he couldn't live in the homo… homophobic South anymore. He was moving and Mark could move with him or not. But there was more to it than that. Mark thought Tony was too controlling. Oh, someone will have to tell Tony." She looked terrified at the thought of having to tell others that her son was dead.

"I can do that if you'd like. I have to talk with him anyway."

"You can't think he had anything to do with this? Tony loved Mark. I know he did. They stayed friends. I think that's why Mark hadn't found anyone else; he kept hoping they'd get back together."

"Do you have a number where Tony can be reached?"

"He moved down to south Florida. Somewhere near Miami. He called me on my birthday." She pulled out her phone and handed it to me. "I barely know how to use this phone. But my birthday was a month ago. October twelfth."

I took the phone and looked at the recents. Most of the calls were from a 251 area code. She had called it two dozen times or more last week. I asked her if that was her son's number, and she nodded. I wrote it down. I found the only Miami area code on her phone on October twelfth and jotted it down next to her son's number.

"Your husband said that you all lived in Florida at one time?"

"Yes, Mark grew up here."

"In Adams County?"

"We lived in an old neighborhood in Calhoun." She rattled off the address and I wrote it down. "We moved to Texas after Mark went off to college. My husband got a job offer out there."

"Just a few more questions. Do you know of anyone that wanted to hurt your son? Anyone who had a grievance against him? Or anyone Mark was afraid of?"

All negative. I told her I would have more questions for her, and she assured me she would answer any questions if it would help to find his killer.

Sitting across from Mark's father, I saw a man who was filled with rage. *Could he kill his son?* That seemed unlikely. Anyway, why would he travel all the way to Florida to do it?

He showed no emotion when we talked about his son. It wasn't until I asked him about their time in Adams County that he seemed to come alive.

"Those were good years. Mark was normal then. He dated girls, played baseball. There was none of that homo crap. My wife was different then too. He changed and then she changed. And who the hell did they blame? Me. That's who. How the hell? I didn't become a queer. He did." He seemed to relax, having blown off some steam. Kemper was wound way too tight.

"Did Mark have any enemies when you all lived here?"

He seemed to be thinking about my question. "No. I mean, there were some minor things. Just what you expect from kids. When he was in middle school there was a kid he didn't like. They got in a fight. Both of them were suspended. I think for a day, maybe two. But he didn't get into any fights after that. The neighborhood had a lot of kids. Different ages. Mark was younger than most of the kids he hung out with. Of course, he was pretty mature for his age." Did I see a crack in his thick skin? A little bit of pride in his son? This man had led a sad life dictated by his stubborn nature.

After we finished, I walked them back out of the hospital. It was still raining. I watched them walk away, separated by a couple of feet and years of anger.

CHAPTER TEN

I drove over to the Kempers' old address when I got back to Adams County. I hadn't thought about it until I turned onto their street, but their house was only a block over from the arson case. *Maybe this will prove whether there is such a thing as coincidence*, I thought to myself.

I drove slowly by the house. It was small, craftsman-style and apparently lived in and well loved now. The lawn was neatly trimmed, the house recently painted and there was a cute barn-shaped mailbox at the curb.

He hung out with the kids in the neighborhood, they said. *Wonder if that included the Danielses?* I drove over to the arson site and pulled into Mr. Canfield's driveway. He wasn't out on the porch that day, which wasn't surprising with the cold, wet weather. A knock on the door summoned Mrs. Canfield, who ushered me into the living room where Tom was sitting in a recliner wrapped in a blanket.

"Feel like a damn invalid. The physical therapist was here this morning. Now I'm aching all over. Sit down. Mary, get him something to drink."

"No, I'm fine," I assured them. I sat down on the sofa. "I just wanted to ask you a few more questions."

"Funny, that other investigator came over after you were

here and he seemed more interested in what questions you asked than he was about the fire."

"Sorry about that. We're kind of stepping on each other's toes."

"Don't worry. Can't say I liked him that much. What do you want to ask?" He had perked up once we started talking.

"The other night we talked about the kids that used to hang out across the street."

"Yeah."

"Do you remember a young man named Mark Kemper?"

"Maybe... Mary?" He raised his voice, calling his wife into the room. "Mary, do you remember a boy named Mark Kemper?"

She knuckled her forehead and thought. "Yes, younger than most of the ones that hung out there, though. You remember. Blond hair, very polite. Dressed a little too neat. The other kids made fun of him, but not... you know, mean. Just kidding. I think they liked him. They seemed to include him in their activities. One of the girls seemed particularly sweet on him." She turned to Tom. "Don't you remember him?"

"I do now. Like you said, he was the one that would offer to help with groceries and such. I don't remember the girls taking up with him."

"One of them—probably Dell, she was the nice one, but it might have been Margret, I just don't remember—used to hang around him more than the other. I thought they had a thing for each other, but who knows with kids."

I stood up. "I appreciate all the help you've given me. This is actually related to a case I'm working. I may as well tell you since it will be in the paper eventually, and we've notified his next of kin. You might have heard about the body that was found out by the AmMex trucking company?"

"My nephew told me about it," Tom said.

"That was Mark Kemper."

"But what could his childhood have had to do with that?'

"Maybe nothing. I'm just following leads. Again, thank

you for your help. I'll be in touch." I left the Canfields somewhat slack-jawed. I think I left them feeling as if violence was encircling them.

I couldn't resist walking over to the burned-out hulk one more time. Did someone have a vendetta against Mark Kemper? If so, why burn down a house that he used to visit instead of the house he actually lived in? I'd have to check the timing, but was it possible that Mark burned the house down and then was killed? I couldn't remember exactly when the fire was recorded, but that seemed unlikely. I was beginning to think that if I solved one mystery I'd have the answer to the other.

Looking at the remains I remembered the articles I'd read about arson. It's a very difficult crime to investigate. In fact, until the 1990s just about everything fire investigators thought they knew about arson was wrong. I knew that there would be a professional report done by the fire investigators from Tallahassee, but without any injuries or ready suspects this case was going to be given a very low priority. I wondered if Matt was making any serious attempt to investigate it.

I had a bit of a dilemma. I should tell Matt about the connection between the murder and the fire, but I didn't really want to. I thought about just sitting on it and pursuing my own investigation to wherever it might lead. But I couldn't quite square that. Matt really was a pretty good investigator. He might be able to use this information to lead him to a suspect. I knew he would never tell me where he was on the fire investigation, but I couldn't be that petty, not at the expense of my investigation. I called him.

I was a little surprised that he took my call. "Yeah," was his laconic greeting.

"Larry here. I've got some information related to your arson case."

"I thought you were told to lay the hell off my cases."

"It wasn't like that." Not that I hadn't tried to get ahead of him on the case. "I came across this while investigating one of my cases."

"Okay."

"I can meet you someplace."

"Can't you just tell me? Or if it's something I need to see, can't you just leave it on my desk?"

For some reason, I'd wanted to see his face when I told him about the connection, but apparently that wasn't going to happen. "My victim used to spend time at your arson site."

"Really?" He actually sounded interested. "When was this, and how did you find out?"

"The when was when he was a kid, about sixteen years old. The how…"

He interrupted me. "How old was your victim when he was killed?"

"Fifty-one."

"That was over thirty years ago." He raised his voice so loud I took the phone away from my ear.

"I know that. But don't you think it's odd that he's killed the same night a house from his childhood is burned?"

"Are you drunk or crazy? Or is this some sort of stupid joke?"

"No, it's not a joke. I thought you might be interested in the information."

"I'm not. You are the worst damn investigator ever. Jesus." He broke the connection.

Try to help some people, I thought. I was actually glad he hadn't been interested. I didn't want to work with the stupid prick anyway.

Two new cases were waiting on my desk. Both were minor issues that could probably be handled over the phone. I sat down to read over them, planning to get them out of my hands as quickly as possible.

Pete showed up about an hour later as I was closing out the cases. He picked up his own pile of new work and shifted through it.

"How many did you get?" he asked.

"Two new."

"Hell, I got three."

"Remember, I'm the lead on the murder."

"Hmmmm, I don't know about that… Let's see… an assault, a robbery and a burglary." He thumbed through them, tossing one aside. "Okay, that one's crap. The man is always drunk. Filing a report of assault against another candidate for a year's detox. And the officer writing the report couldn't even see any evidence." He looked at the next one. "Robbery is legit, but I know this little peckerwood too and I'll bet you that the ten dollars and fifty cents was only part of what was taken. Can you spell D.R.U.G.S?" He opened the last folder. "Okay, this is odd. Burglary, fairly nice neighborhood and nothing was stolen. Why would someone break in, spend a bit of time and not take anything? Odd. Domestic maybe? This one might require some effort."

"Don't short-change the other two."

"Yeah, I know, I'm being unfair to the alcoholics and the drug addicts. Please, I've got better things to do than help lowlifes get back at one another. Speaking of that murder case, how're things going?"

I filled him in on the victim, the family and the strange connection from the past with the arson.

"That *is* weird. You tell Matt?"

"Of course. He thought I was crazy."

"He ain't one for subtlety. Sounds like you played it right. Now you don't have to sneak around. You've got a clear connection between the two cases. Well, sort of clear."

"I need to call the victim's ex." Not being able to interview him properly, I decided that I wanted to record the conversation. Even if we eliminated him as a suspect, if we went to trial the defendant's lawyer could try to prove that we didn't follow all the available leads, so it was handy if you could pull out a record and prove that you had talked to as many people as possible.

Tony Frye picked up on the second ring. "Hello?" He sounded short of breath.

"Hey, this is Deputy Larry Macklin with the Adams County Sheriff's Office…"

He started crying. "I know. I can't believe it."

"Mr. Frye, I'm going to record our conversation. Do you understand? Is that okay with you?"

He was choking on tears as he answered, "Yes, oh God…"

"So you've already heard that your friend Mark Kemper was found murdered here in Adams County?"

"I called his mother." More crying. "I hadn't gotten a text or a call in a week. I wanted to know what was wrong. I never thought…"

"You all were still close after the breakup?"

"Yes, friends, more than friends. We'd been together for fifteen years. It was me. I'm so stupid. This never would have happened if I hadn't left."

"Do you know who might have done this to him?"

"Oh, oh, no. It couldn't have been done… on purpose. Everybody liked Mark. How… could someone? No. He didn't have any enemies."

"Are you sure? Sometimes people can get mad about stupid things. Are you sure he didn't mention any problems with someone?"

"No, he never had any trouble with people. He always wanted to make things right. That's what he'd say. I just want to make things right with people."

"I'm sorry, but I need to know where you were on Monday night a week ago."

"You're kidding me." He was sputtering and crying. "How dare you? I loved that man. I never would have done anything to hurt him."

"Please, Mr. Frye, understand my position. I don't know either one of you or anything about your relationship. Now, if you could just tell me where you were on Monday night a week ago." Interviews like this were difficult at best to do over the phone. Of course we didn't have the money or manpower to send me down to Miami for a routine questioning. Get a serious suspect and you could get authorization pretty quick, but just to make it easier on a deputy and a grieving friend, no.

"Yes, I know… It's just hurtful that anyone would think… Miami, I was working at the Rainbow Wind Bar. I know," he said wearily. "Dumbest name ever. I'm the manager. We do karaoke Mondays. Lots of people saw me."

"Sorry I had to ask." I made a note of the name. I'd have to call down there and verify his alibi. "So you can't think of any reason someone would want to harm Mark?"

"No, really, just no. The only person he didn't get along with was his father. But they hadn't talked in years. When… Do you know if… I mean, a memorial service?"

"His parents will be making all of the arrangements. I don't see why the body can't be released immediately."

"I'll get the information from his mother."

"I'm sorry for your loss."

"I am too," he said and disconnected us.

CHAPTER ELEVEN

My watch said six o'clock by the time I'd finished doing paperwork and emails, including sending one to Dahlia thanking her for her help and letting her know that we had found Mark's family. Ivy was going to be wondering where I was.

As I passed the front desk on my way out, an older woman, the type who maintains shadows of her beauty well into middle age, was talking to the desk sergeant.

"I know it's probably too late to speak with anyone, but I wanted to let Mr. Greene know that I'm in town." Her face was kind. Her high cheekbones and strong chin were tempered by her soft eyes.

"He's working a case for you?" the desk sergeant asked in a disinterested voice.

"I'm Dell McDonnell. Our house burned down," she said with an air of sadness.

I stopped and went over to the desk. "Maybe I can help." They both looked at me with gratitude.

"You're Deputy Greene?" she asked.

"No, but I'm a... colleague." I'd almost said friend. "I can take some information and pass it on to him. I'm sure he'll contact you tomorrow."

"That would be great." She smiled tiredly. "I drove down from Georgia and I'm exhausted."

"Come on in and sit down, and we can talk for a minute." She followed me back to a small conference room just past the sheriff's office.

"Can I get you something to drink? Coffee? Water?"

"No, I'm fine," she said, sitting down at the table. "Mr. Greene said on the phone that it was probably arson? Why would someone do that?"

"Honestly, we can't say that it's arson yet. It can be very tricky determining whether the fire was set or if something like newspapers or rags spontaneously combusted. It didn't appear to be an electrical fire. We've sent samples off to the lab. They'll check them for signs of any accelerant, gasoline, kerosene, something like that. The fact that no one was living there is the primary reason we suspect arson."

"I had cleaned out most of the junk that Momma had collected. But there were still photo albums and newspaper clippings. Some clothes. Oh, it's horrible to think that we've lost all of that. I should have cleaned it out after we got Momma up to our place. I just never found the time."

"Don't blame yourself. Can you think of anyone that might have a grudge against your family?"

She looked surprised by the question. "Really... I... no. No. Momma always got along with her neighbors. Even when she was getting pretty dotty it was always in a nice way. She went to the wrong house a few times, but no one seemed to mind. In fact, I think they were all worried about her. It's a real nice neighborhood with good people."

"Maybe someone from your family's past?"

This caused her to look straight into my eyes. "From our past? That seems like an odd question." Some of the tiredness had left her. I'd definitely gotten her attention.

"It's probably an unrelated case, but it's something else we're looking into. Do you remember a young man by the name of Mark Kemper?" As soon as I said the name there was a flash of emotion in her eyes, but I couldn't tell what it was.

"Well... maybe," she said, oddly stalling her answer. "I think there was a boy. Might have come around our house some." Curiouser and curiouser. "Is this Mark Kemper involved in something?" She straightened up in the chair and her hands were now holding each other.

In for a penny, in for a pound, I thought. "Mark Kemper was found dead the morning after the fire at your house."

"But I thought..." She stopped herself. What had she thought? "He's dead? What happened to him?"

"He was murdered." Now there was panic in her eyes. What the hell did she know?

"If you know anything about this, it's important that you tell me." She knew I knew that she knew something.

"I'm really very tired. I'd rather get some rest right now and I'll be glad to talk to you and Mr. Greene tomorrow."

I put my hands out to her. "Please. This could be very important. A man was murdered."

"I have to think. Really, I don't think I know anything that could help you, but I need some time to think."

She got up and seemed confused. All of the exhaustion she'd been feeling before looked like it had doubled and settled down on her shoulders. I know when an interview is over. I opened the door for her and escorted her out of the building.

"Thank you for talking with me. If you want to talk before tomorrow, just call me. Anytime." I handed her my card.

How the hell was I going to explain this to Matt? He was going to be furious. The worst part was I knew he had every right to be pissed. Getting in my car, I decided I'd wait and talk to him first thing in the morning.

At home, Ivy wove in and out of my legs, almost tripping me as I fed her dinner. She purred and ate as I fixed myself a bowl of soup. After the wet, cold and depressing day I'd had, I needed something warm.

I started to reread William Manchester's *The Glory and the*

Dream and fell asleep thinking about the trials and tribulations of the greatest generation.

Before I even left the house in the morning I texted Matt: *Talked to Dell McDonnell. Let's meet and discuss.* The response was fast and succinct: *See you in 30.*

He was waiting for me in the lobby.

"In here," he said. I followed him to the same conference room where I'd talked to Dell.

I hadn't gotten the door closed when he started yelling.

"What the hell? Didn't you understand what I said the other day? What'd I say? Stay the hell away from my case. That's it. Just 'cause your daddy's the sheriff doesn't give you the right to step the crap all over my work."

I let him blow off steam then said as calmly as I could, "I explained that our cases might be linked."

"Go to hell and you can take your damn link." Okay, letting off steam might not be enough. This might turn into a full-on boiler explosion.

"You weren't here. I saw her at the desk when I was leaving and offered to talk to her. That's all."

"No, that's not all, you…" He pulled back on the last insult, which I took as a good sign.

"You could have called me or texted me. I would have come back," he said.

Unfortunately I knew that to be true. Matt worked his cases and actually was much more committed to the job than I ever was or probably ever would be. I held up my hands in surrender. For a minute I thought I might have made a huge mistake when he pulled back and started to throw a punch at my face. But he didn't follow through and that seemed to break the fever. Now he was just pacing back and forth.

"Okay, screw you. What'd she say?"

"She didn't know anything about the fire and didn't know of any enemies that she or her family had." Now I had to decide whether I told him about her reaction to my victim's name. I was starting to feel guilty for not giving him the first chance to question her. "There was one thing."

Matt looked me square in the eyes for the first time. I went on. "She reacted strongly when I mentioned my victim's name and told her that he'd been murdered the night of the fire."

"So you said that he was an old friend of the family? Couldn't she have been upset to find out that a friend had died?"

"Yeah, but right before that I'd asked her if she knew a Mark Kemper and she acted like she wanted to deny it."

He cocked his head to one side, a habit he had when he was thinking about something. "Okay, maybe, and I mean a very big maybe, there *is* some kind of link here. You think he started the fire and then someone killed him?"

"The timing is close. It might be possible. Or maybe my shooter started the fire and then shot Kemper. Though that seems odd. Kemper doesn't even live in the state. How and why would the shooter entice Kemper here to shoot him? Why do it on the same night as the fire?"

"Usually if you have a murder and a fire, the fire is set to cover up the murder," he said didactically.

"But you see the reasoning behind thinking the two might be linked?"

"Maybe. I'll talk to Dell McDonnell and see what I can get."

"She had more to say about my victim, that's for sure. I'd like to be present when you interview her."

He looked like he was going to give me a snappy answer, but reconsidered. "Okay, but I take the lead." Matt was a good investigator and I was seeing that he could put his feelings aside for a case.

"Appreciate that," I said, trying to cover the hatchet over with as much dirt as possible.

Matt said he'd get up with her and let me know when they would meet.

In the meantime, I decided to take care of some

paperwork and then go out and find my new confidential informant, one Mister Eddie Thompson.

Pete was working a couple of his cases and cleaning up the paperwork. I interrupted long enough to give him the short version of where we were on the Kemper case.

"Those two cases tied together... how awkward for you and Matt," he said, smiling as he took a break from his computer to grab a piece of leftover Halloween candy from another investigator's desk.

"Yeah, thanks," I said, rubbing my middle finger against the side of my head and making sure that he saw the motion.

"Love you, kid. Now I have grown-up work to do," Pete said, wheeling back to his computer.

"I'm going out. Call me if you need anything."

On my way out to my car I tried calling Eddie and got his voicemail.

"Eddie, this is your new best friend calling. I'd like to talk about our partnership. Call me or I'll find you."

I drove out to AmMex. If he was there he'd see that I was serious about hunting him down. I wouldn't make contact there, but I wanted him to know that I wasn't fooling around.

The wind had shifted out of the north. The skies were clearing and the temperature dropping. I didn't see him as I drove through the parking lot, but less than ten minutes later my phone rang.

"What are you doing, man? I told you I'd call. We can't be seen together."

"This long-distance relationship isn't working for me."

"I've heard things. Seriously. I'm trying to follow up."

"I want something soon, or I'm going to haul your panty-clad ass into jail."

"That's not cool, man."

"What's not cool is making a bargain and not holding up your end. You need to feed me something. I'm getting hungry and when I get hungry I'm not always careful about what I eat. Get me?" I was actually enjoying the bad cop dialogue.

"Whatever. I'll get up with you tomorrow."

"Don't screw me over." I hung up on him.

My phone rang again and for a minute I thought Eddie was calling me back to engage in more cops-and-robbers talk. But then I saw it was Matt and figured he was calling about a meeting with Dell. He was, but it wasn't exactly how I imagined.

"I'm at the Roads Best Motel at the interstate. You need to come down here now." The tone of his voice made it clear that asking questions would just be a waste of time.

"I'll be there in ten minutes."

CHAPTER TWELVE

I made tracks to the motel, turning up my dispatch radio as I drove. I'd gotten into the bad habit of turning it down when I was talking on the phone and not bothering to turn it back up. I called in to the office and told them where I was heading. Listening to the radio, I had a good idea what I was going to find when I got there.

Crime scene vans from our department and the state blocked a section of the motel's parking lot. Yellow crime scene tape was strewn here and there, marking off different areas to be photographed, videotaped and searched for evidence.

Matt's short dark form stood by the railing on the second floor. He didn't turn to look at me as I walked up the metal and concrete steps.

He pulled his coat in tight against the north wind and said, "Two motels at the interstate and she had to pick the cheap-ass one that doesn't have interior hallways or working security cameras. What'd she save, twenty dollars? Jesus."

I had nothing to add to that so I walked around him and went to the door of room 225 and peered inside. The body lay on the bed, still dressed in the clothes she'd been wearing when I saw her the night before. The only thing different was that her forehead and face were a bloody pulp. I tried to see if she still had her fingers, though I couldn't imagine why the killer would have taken the fingers of Mrs. McDonnell.

"The fingers are there, honey," Shantel said when she saw me looking at the corpse. She looked like a strange doll dressed in her disposable crime scene protection clothing. "And get your hair-shedding, nasty head back outside that door. It comes in here, it better be wearing something to protect my crime scene. Or it will be looking like hers." She waved at Dell's bloody and battered head. I dutifully took my head out of the doorway and walked back over to Matt.

"Guess *we* have a murder case now."

He turned and looked at me for the first time. "Unless you want to fight about it."

"If I fought you, it would be to give you *both* Kemper's and McDonnell's cases," I told him.

"No, thanks. 'Sides, you were right on the arson crossover."

I almost fell over from shock. Matt Greene said I was right!

"So how do you want to do this?" I threw it out there because I knew he must be considering the options too.

"Yeah, we need to come up with a system so we aren't stepping all over each other's dicks."

We weren't partner material, so working too closely was out. "Look, we can create an interview list together. Divide it up, each taking a share. If we come up with a possible suspect, we interview him or her together."

"Yeah, that's part of it. How about the direction of the investigation?"

"We need to come to an agreement. If we can't, we present our competing ideas to Lt. Johnson and he decides."

"Okay, we'll try that. Might work," he said without conviction.

"All we can do is try."

"One more thing… Don't let that donut-swilling partner of yours get near me."

I didn't say anything in response to that. Defending Pete to Matt wouldn't do any good. There was some serious bad blood there. Five years ago, when Matt was still on the road, he had made a routine traffic stop. The driver of the car came out with a gun before Matt was all the way out of his patrol car. I've seen the video from Matt's patrol car, and the speed with which it all went down was terrifying. Matt fell over backward, trying to draw his gun and put distance between himself and the shooter. Unfortunately, as Matt went down he lost control of his handgun and it went flying across the asphalt into the darkness.

At that point all Matt could do was run like hell. Since he was young and fast, and the shooter was stupid and drunk, Matt didn't get shot. But he was screaming for help over his radio, begging for assistance. When help finally arrived the suspect was found sitting in his car with an empty revolver. He dropped the gun when told to, which is the only reason he made it to trial.

But the animosity between Pete and Matt stemmed from the investigation into the incident. Dad appointed three senior officers to review the event in order to come up with recommendations to ensure that our deputies wouldn't be caught in a similar situation. As part of the investigation, a timeline of the locations of all deputies on duty that night was created. As it turned out, the nearest deputy to the incident was Pete, who didn't have his radio turned up loud enough to hear Matt's screams for help. He had called in that he was going on break, but most deputies keep their radios on loud enough to at least hear when something really bad is going down. Pete, however, was in a conversation with one of the locals at the donut shop up the road and never heard the "officer in trouble" call.

Matt had had a vendetta against Pete ever since. The mere idea that while he was scrambling for his life Pete was eating donuts right up the road made it impossible for Matt to even acknowledge Pete whenever they passed in the hall. Pete took it pretty hard at first, feeling guilty. But how long can you feel bad? Matt didn't get hurt and Pete learned a lesson. But Matt couldn't let it go.

"Flip you a coin to see who calls the husband." Matt was completely serious.

"No, I talked to her last night. Naturally, he'll want to know about our meeting. I'll do it."

Matt nodded. He pulled out his phone and found some notes he'd made. "You want to do it now?"

I sighed and nodded. He held the phone up so I could see the number. "That's the number I reached her at. It's a landline, so it must be their home number."

I dialed it on my phone and waited, thinking about what Mr. Canfield said about Dell caring for her mother. Who was going to take care of her now? After a few rings, Mr. McDonnell answered. I made sure that he wasn't alone—a daughter was there with him helping to take care of Dell's mother. Maybe that answered that question. I told him what had happened as sparingly as possible. He took it as well as anyone can when they get devastating news. I ended up speaking to the daughter, who seemed almost too calm and managed to ask the right questions. Arrangements would be made. Someone would come down, etc., etc. Finally it was over. I put the phone back on my hip.

After I had time to recover from the call, Matt turned to me. "This one," he said.

"What?"

"He or she planned the first murder so they were careful. There's no real evidence at the arson either, but this murder… This looks sloppy. The killer didn't have time to think about how he was going to do it. He might have known on his way over here, but he didn't have a lot of time to get organized. So McDonnell's murder is the best chance of finding good evidence."

"That makes sense." Evidence found at the scene is one way to find a suspect. "But I think we need to find the motive. These are three very different crimes, yet we know that they're linked. So if we can find the person who had a motive to commit all three of them, that will give us a prime suspect. Then we can look for the evidence to link him to the crime scenes."

Matt nodded. "I'll follow up on the evidence, including going back over the crime scene at the warehouse and all the material collected there. You go over all the people who have a connection to the three crimes. We'll see who comes up with a suspect first." He seemed almost pleased at the idea of us engaging in some type of *mano a mano* contest of skills. Whatever.

"Sure." I heard gunshots. It was Dad's ringtone on my phone.

"Jesus, dumbass." Matt had flinched when the ringtone went off.

"Hello," I said to my dad.

"Yeah, so you let another person get murdered." That was Dad's sense of humor. "Understand from Johnson that there's a connection between the Kemper murder and this one. But this one is also connected to Matt's arson? When you're done at the crime scene, come in and tell me where we are on these." This was an order.

"Greene's here so I can come now if you want."

"Good."

I hung up and told Matt that the sheriff wanted an update. "You can do it if you want," I said seriously.

"No." I could tell that he wanted to make a snide remark in a nepotistic vein, but was resisting the urge with difficulty.

"Call if you need anything," I said sincerely.

I was escorted right into Dad's office. I dropped down on one of the two leather-bound chairs that face his Olympic-size desk. The desk was mostly covered with awards and trinkets from junkets. There was a small pile of files on current cases, a keyboard and a monitor. He glanced up when I sat down. He knew better than to expect me to stand at his desk as though I wasn't his son and hadn't seen him a thousand times shuffling around in his robe or snoring away on the sofa.

"Two real murders." I knew that by "real" he meant "not drug related." "Do we have a suspect?"

"We don't even have suspects plural," I told him and received a frown in return.

"Neither of the victims actually lived here now, right?" He was hopeful that he could spin this as non-county residents being killed by non-county residents... Nothing for a voter to be concerned about. He took his job of protecting the citizens of the county very seriously, but there was a part of him that resented people from outside the county coming here and committing crimes or being a victim. He thought they were purposely trying to screw up his crime rate.

"Both lived out of state, but as you know they both have roots here in the county."

Another frown. "Do we need to devote more resources to this?" That was Dad-speak for *If you can't handle this, I'll find someone who can.*

"I think Matt and I can do this."

"Can you two work together?"

"We'll put 'kick me' signs on each other's backs every chance we get, but I think we can put most of our differences aside long enough to solve these murders and the arson."

"Are we definitely thinking that it's a single perp?"

"I'm ninety-nine percent sure."

"Greene agree with you?" Dad-speak for *I don't trust you. Tell me what someone I do trust thinks.*

"Yes. He does now."

"Oh, yeah, you thought there was a link between your murder and his arson in the first place." Dad-speak for *I can't believe a dumbass like you managed to be right for once.* "One more thing. Don't talk to the press. Have them call my office if they want any information."

"Sure. I'll pass that along to Matt."

"He's not dumb enough to talk to the press." Boy, the

implication there was clear. Finally he said, "Okay." Which was sheriff-speak for *Go away.*

"Nice chat. How's everything going in your life?" I said. He ignored the sarcasm.

"Mauser seemed a little gimpy on his front leg this morning."

"I could take him to the vet," I offered too quickly.

He put down the papers he'd been holding and looked me square in the face for the first time since I'd come into the office. "Why are you in such a hurry to take Mauser to the vet?"

"Trying to help, that's all," I said. He didn't believe a word of it.

He went back to the report he was reading and I went to the door. Once outside his office, though, I turned around and knocked.

"What?" came his standard reply. I opened the door and walked back in. Dad gave me a look between *What the hell?* and *Why the hell?* "Forget something?"

"Actually, Sheriff, I need to ask you a few questions." I caught him short by calling him Sheriff.

Off guard, he asked, "What are you talking about?"

"I went out and came back in in an effort to get us into investigator/interviewee mode, separate from the father/son thing."

"What are you talking about?"

"Well, we talked about you knowing the Daniels family."

"Yeah."

"Do you recognize the name Mark Kemper?"

He sat back, looking at me. "Should I?" He was interested now.

"Mark Kemper used to hang out at the Daniels house too."

"Really." He got a thoughtful look in his eyes. "Maybe."

"He would have been younger than most of you by about two or three years. Blond hair."

"Dressed nice all the time. Real polite. Yeah, I do

remember. That's your other dead body?"

"Yes."

"Strange."

"Mark, the house and Dell. They have to be linked, and you and your gang are probably part of the connection."

"That's a stretch, but I can certainly see where you're coming from. Interesting."

"So where were you last night?" I said it calmly with the same seriousness I would have asked any suspect.

He narrowed his eyes. "I guess you have the right to ask. Well, Deputy, I was at home most of the evening. I got two calls from the duty officer. One was about the detention of an inebriated county commissioner who had attempted to get in his car and drive, but was detained, first by the owner of the bar, who had called us when the commissioner became violent with him, then by one of our deputies who suffered much verbal abuse from the commissioner. The other call was about a break-in at the hardware store on Main. They wanted authorization to call in some off-duty officers to help track the suspects who were on the run through a residential neighborhood. There will be a record of both calls."

"Handled through your cell phone?"

"Yes. Except for the two calls, my only alibi is Mauser. Now on the first night, I was at a meeting of the Chamber of Commerce and didn't leave until after midnight. So that should clear me of the first murder." Amazingly, he said this without any sarcasm.

"Do you have any idea what the connection between these three events could be?"

"No. I'm trying to think of who else hung out there. Of course it might not have to do with that time period. You're going to have to do some digging to find out if there is another time when all three elements came together.

"Let's see… Of course there was Jim, Margret, Dell and me. The four of us made up the core group. Mark started hanging around when Jim, Margret and I were in our senior year. Dell was one year younger, so she must have been a junior. You can eliminate Mr. and Mrs. Daniels. He's dead and she has dementia. A couple of other kids came around some. I mentioned Fred, but he's dead too. There was a guy, David, big fella, played football. He left as soon as the girls made it clear that neither of them was interested in him. I've got my yearbooks at the house. I'll go through them and see what other names I can get you."

His interest was piqued and he wasn't pissed that I'd been a little snarky about him being a suspect. It was a good time to leave. "I'll come by this evening and we can go through them."

"Sounds good," he said and I headed for the door, leaving him visiting the past and looking dreamy.

I went to my desk and called Tim Devries. "How's your dad?" I asked.

"Same. Not good. Hey, don't worry, I haven't gotten into any more fights with my sister."

"That wasn't why I was calling. I need your mother's phone number." I don't think I sounded demanding, but even over the phone I could tell he bowed up a little.

"Why?"

"There was a murder last night and another one a week ago. Oddly, your father, mine and your mother knew both of the victims. I just need to talk to her and see if she knows anyone that might have wanted them dead."

"She might not answer. The woman is almost always on some shopping spree or getting a spa treatment or some other expensive crap. And honestly doesn't give a damn about anybody but herself." It sounded like he was trying to convince me not to bother calling her.

"I'm going to give it a try."

"I'll have to get the number." More stalling?

"It isn't on your phone?"

"Yeah, I guess. I don't talk to her very often. Hold on, I'll look." Silence for a minute and then he rattled off the number while I wrote it down.

"Thanks."

"Yeah," he said and hung up.

I decided to wait before calling Margret Devries. I wanted to have my questions well thought out. I looked over at Matt's desk and saw the arson file was sitting on top of a pile of reports. I had the right to look at it now, so I went over and picked it up, brought it back to my desk and started reading through it again. There were a few more notes and another preliminary report from the state fire marshal's office.

The fire seemed like the outlier. Explain why the house had to be burned down, and we might have a line on a suspect. The fire appeared to have started near a chest of drawers filled with photos and old papers. Was someone trying to destroy the papers? If you believed that the fire could have started naturally, then it made some sense that it started where there were old papers that could have spontaneously ignited. Once the fire started, flashover occurred within the first ten minutes. Not unusual. No obvious indications of an accelerant, but they were still waiting on lab tests. Blah, blah, blah.

The only thing that might mean anything was where the fire started. I decided to make my third trip out to the house. Heading out the door, I almost bumped into Pete coming in.

"You busy?"

He looked toward his desk. "Why?"

"I'm heading out to the arson site. Want to ride along?"

It didn't take him long to decide that riding around with me would be better than facing the reports on his desk.

CHAPTER THIRTEEN

Outside the north wind was strong and cold. The weathermen were saying this was going to be the coldest weather so far this year.

First, I swung by the newest crime scene. They were just finishing up. Matt had gone for lunch. Unfortunately they hadn't found any big clues like a dropped phone, watch or a lost coat button. But since it was a motel room they'd found a ton of latent prints and hair and fiber evidence that would have to be sorted through.

At the site of the arson, Pete waited outside the ruins while I stumbled through the burned-out hulk, trying to identify where the reports indicated the fire had started. I knew nothing about fires. I had never wanted to be a fireman. The idea of running toward a burning building always struck me as insane. While I wasn't too keen on the job I had and arguably wasn't that good at it, I could not imagine fighting fires for a living. They are braver men than me.

Finally I found the suspected ignition spot. The chest of drawers was almost completely destroyed, but picking through the pieces I found scraps of paper and old pictures that had managed to survive the worst of the fire. Nothing was very legible. You could tell that they were bills, newspaper clippings or remains of photographs, but nothing more. It seemed that a mish-mash of memorabilia had been stored here. I even found part of an old passport. Dell might have made some sense of it, but I certainly couldn't. Was that one of the reasons she had been killed?

"Nice neighborhood," Pete said as I climbed out of the wreckage.

"There is, or was, something rotten in Denmark," I said. "I'm pretty sure something that started here has ended in two murders."

"Weird when you look around. It looks like any other neighborhood."

"That's what's so terrifying. It *is* like any other neighborhood.

"There's an old guy who lives a block over. Korean War vet, he's got a silver and two bronze stars. I help him out sometimes. He's been living here for a long time. Might know something. At least he could point out other old-timers. I'll follow up on any leads he gives me."

"Works for me."

"I come up with anything, you probably won't want to let Matt know where the lead came from," he said remorsefully.

"Sooner or later you two are going to have to settle the issue."

"Last time I tried, I thought he was going to slug me. You know, I'd really feel bad if I had to Taser his ass." Pete shook his head. "It's not just 'cause I was at the donut shop. He's projecting a lot of his anger onto me because he was embarrassed that he lost his gun and had to run into the woods."

"You're right. But I wouldn't point that out to him," I said, shaking my head.

Later, I found Matt doing paperwork on the McDonnell murder. He didn't have any more info than what I got from the crime techs earlier. Tomorrow he planned on sitting in on the autopsy. Which, contrary to TV, is not something we routinely do. But Matt had a background in medicine and spent time taking courses in forensic studies. Honestly, if he wasn't such a prick he'd be working for a much bigger agency. He'd applied to the FBI and the DEA. He never told us where the application processes broke down, but I've always believed it was the interviews. I could almost feel sorry for him.

It was almost five o'clock. I decided that I wanted to tackle Margret Devries before I went home. Half hoping I'd get her voicemail, I dialed the number Tim gave me. She picked up on the third ring.

"Who is this?" *Who answers their phone like that?* As sweet as her sister's voice had been, Margret's was grating.

"This is Deputy Larry Macklin, I'm calling about…"

"About time someone from your office called me. My sister's husband has already informed me of her murder. Why wasn't I called?"

"It isn't customary for us to call all of the deceased's relatives." I already didn't like her… at all. Not one bit.

"I want to speak with the sheriff."

"I'm one of the officers investigating your sister's murder."

"Why isn't the sheriff taking the lead?" Her voice was rising with every question she asked and every unsatisfactory answer she received.

I wanted to say because he has more important things to do. But that wouldn't have been the honest answer, and it wouldn't have been the right answer to give to someone you were planning on interviewing. So I dug deep for a response that wouldn't sink any opportunity at cooperation from Mrs. Devries. "He is overseeing this case. Sheriff Macklin is personally involved with every important case that the Adams County Sheriff's Office handles."

"Then I'd like to talk to him directly."

"I'm very sorry, but he's meeting with the coroner and

several other county and state officials, pulling in all the resources he can to find the person that killed your sister. He told me to apologize for not contacting you personally. But we need as much information as we can get, as quickly as possible, and if you could answer a few questions it would be a big help." I don't think that I could have layered on any more bullshit.

"Never mind, I'm on my way there right now. I told Dell's husband I would oversee the arrangements and find out what was being done to hunt down the maniac who killed her. Tell the sheriff I'll be at his office first thing in the morning." She hung up.

While I would have loved letting Dad walk into that maelstrom without prior warning, I couldn't really allow that to happen. I texted him that I would be over to his place as soon as I stopped by mine, fed Ivy and changed clothes. *I'm leaving here in 30. See you at the house* was the response I got back.

I let myself into Dad's house and called out for him. I received just one window-rattling bark from Mauser and a "right there" from Dad. In the living room I settled into a chair, hoping that Mauser would stay on the couch. No luck. He came over, sniffed Ivy's scent, turned, backed up and sat in my lap. To Mauser humans had several functions—to feed him, to let him out or in and to be furniture.

Dad came in and ruffled Mauser's head.

"What's up?" he said, sitting down in his recliner. Mauser got up and went to get a treat from Dad, who duly placated the monster. By the grace of God the dog decided that my lap wasn't that comfortable and laid down on the sofa. I did notice that when he went to the sofa he favored his right front leg a little.

"He's still a little gimpy," Dad said.

I decided to play it cool and was rewarded when Dad asked, "You know your offer to take him to the vet? Would you mind? I'm booked solid for tomorrow."

"I can make time in the afternoon," I said easily. "Your schedule tomorrow is part of the reason I'm here. I talked to Margret Devries and she's coming over from Jacksonville. She doesn't want to talk to me either. She said she wanted you to personally handle the case and she's coming to see you in the morning."

"Damn it. Can't you deal with her? Never mind, I know what she can be like. She almost drove poor Jim to Chattahoochee. I'll meet with her briefly. You be there too, and I'll make it as clear as possible that you and Greene are in charge of the case. I can play up the fact that you're my son, which shows that I'm taking it very personally."

"Good luck."

He huffed and went into a back room, coming out with three yearbooks. We sat at the dining room table and went through them. It was heart-wrenching to see pictures of my mom. She and Dad didn't get together until his first year at college, so there were no pictures of them together. He pointed out a couple kids that had come by from time to time, but none of them were a part of the group, and he couldn't imagine that they would have a reason from back then to kill someone today.

When I got to the office Wednesday morning, the desk sergeant told me that Margret Devries was already there. I waited for Matt and Dad to show up before I went anywhere near the woman. I figured this needed to be a shared experience.

Mrs. Devries, tall and well rounded with a face that showed signs of professional work, stood pacing back and forth in front of Dad's office. Matt and I let him take the lead.

"Ted Macklin? I'd forgotten you were sheriff," Margret said as he got within shouting distance.

"I am. If you'll let us get in my office, we can talk about

your sister's case." He maneuvered around her and opened his office door, holding it for her. One of Dad's talents was diplomacy when he wanted to use it.

"What have you learned about my sister's murder?" she demanded, invading his personal space. Dad eased around his desk, putting some acreage between them.

"These are Deputies Greene and Macklin," he said. "They are the men working the case for me." Dad tried to deflect her attention onto us. It didn't work.

"You're the sheriff, aren't you? Why should I have to listen to your lackeys? Don't you know what's going on?" She tried to stare him down.

Dad met her gaze. "I'm telling you that these men have firsthand knowledge of the case. Wouldn't you rather hear the details of the investigation directly from them rather than get it second hand from me?"

She thought about this for a moment. "Why aren't you directly involved?"

"Would you rather have the owner of the restaurant prepare your dinner or the chef?"

He'd finally found an argument that she seemed to think held merit. Reluctantly she turned to Matt and me. "Okay, what do you two know about my sister's killer?"

Before we could answer there was a knock at the door. Exasperated, Dad called out, "What?"

The door opened and an assistant stuck her head in. "Sorry to interrupt, but Tim Devries is here and would like to hear anything you have to say to his mother."

"I have a right," Tim said, loud enough for all of us in the office to hear him.

"Show him in," Dad said in a voice that was too calm.

"But…" Mrs. Devries started to say, but Dad cut her off.

"Can't hurt for him to join us." He said it fast before she could say anything more.

Tim pushed past the assistant. "Mom, you should have talked to me before you came here."

"I don't have to talk to you about anything. How did you

even find out I was in town? Let me guess, Little Miss Motor Mouth." And, as if on cue, the door opened again and Tilly pushed her way in, despite the assistant's best attempts to block her.

"I told you I'd handle this," said Tim at the same time that her mother said, "I told you not to tell anyone..."

Dad lifted both his hands above his head. "Enough! It is too early in the morning for this crap!" To emphasize his point, he slammed his hands down on the desk. "Everyone sit down!"

No one felt like arguing with him, so we all found something to sit on. Dad eased himself down in his big leather chair and eyed Tim and Tilly.

"You two have seen fit to barge into my office." He held up a hand to stop them from saying anything in their defense. "I'm sure that you want to see your aunt's killer brought to justice and that you are also here out of concern for your mother." I wasn't so sure that the latter part was true. "So since this meeting was requested by your mother, I'll let her decide if she wants you all to sit in on it."

Everyone looked at Margret Devries. "What the hell, you're all here anyway." She gritted her teeth and looked around at us. "Now, will someone tell me how close you are to finding my sister's killer?"

Matt surprised me again by leaning forward and facing off with the woman.

"We aren't very far into the investigation. I'm going to the autopsy this afternoon. Maybe we will get some idea of the type of blunt object used to damage her face. And possibly we'll discover that there was another, different, cause of death, say strangulation, and that the pulverizing of the facial features was done post-mortem. But... and this is my point... These things take time."

"Thank you, Greene. He's right. If we don't find the murderer standing over the body then we have to move forward the best we can, and with caution so that we don't inadvertently damage our chances of prosecuting a suspect when we have one."

I decided I should put in my two cents. "The assumption that we are currently working with is that this murder is connected to the murder of Mark Kemper." I paused to see if this would have the same effect on Margret that it did on Dell. She showed no reaction, which I found curious. "You did know Mark Kemper?"

She looked at me as though I was a dead fish she had found in her bed. "I'm sure I didn't."

"We're sure you did."

"How dare you accuse me of lying?" She was doing her best offended dowager routine, but I really wasn't buying it.

Dad stepped in. "You remember Mark. He started hanging around your house when we were seniors. You must have been a junior at the time."

She looked over at him, her face showing annoyance. "There were a lot of wannabes hanging around our house in those days. Dell and I were two of the prettiest girls at Adams County High School."

And modest too, I wanted to add.

"Maybe there was a Mark, now that you mention it. Blond hair, he was very young."

"Now he's dead," I emphasized.

"This all seems like a crazy conspiracy theory or something," Tim said. "It sounds to me like there is some whack job going around beating people to death."

I looked over at Tilly, whose eyes were going back and forth, following the speakers. Finally she spoke. "Yeah, why can't you find this guy? How many psychopathic killers are there running around this county? Can't you find the one that murdered my aunt?"

I almost laughed out loud, but constrained myself. These people were nuts. "It's not quite so easy as going around and checking to see where all the psychopathic killers were on the night of the crimes."

Dad stepped in. "We've been running background checks on the all the violent felons that might be living in the area."

Tilly gave me a "see there" look.

"So when will you arrest someone?" Margret asked.

"We have some evidence which, for the sake of the investigation, we can't share. It is going to take a while to fully develop it and to determine in which direction it points. Until that time, we will keep the families of all the victims informed of the progress of the investigation." Dad rattled this off and then looked at the Devries family with the profound hope that they would take the hint and leave. No such luck.

"I don't think you all are trying," Margret stated flatly.

Tim stepped in. "Mom, why don't you let me liaison with the sheriff on this. You have Aunt Dell's funeral arrangements to deal with."

The reminder about the funeral seemed to redirect her mind. "So much has been placed on my shoulders."

"That seems like a great way for us to move forward," Dad said judiciously. There was no doubt that dealing with Tim would be much, much more preferable to ever having to talk to Margret Devries again.

"That might be best until I've dealt with this funeral. But as soon as it's done, I'm going to want answers and someone locked up for my sister's brutal murder."

"I'll work closely with them. I'm sure that they are doing everything they can to find the murderer," Tim said.

"You've always been like your father, too naïve." She turned and, without another word, stormed out of the office.

"Sorry about my mom. She's… headstrong. Which one of you will I be working with on my aunt's case?" Tim looked around the room.

"Why don't you and my son work together?" Dad gestured toward me.

"I'll be in touch." He shook my hand with a firm manly grip, the kind you would expect from a man who'd worked on the land beside his dad most of his life.

"Fine, and I'll call you if there is any new information about the case that we can share," I told him.

"You've always been a suck up," Tilly said to Tim as she followed him out of Dad's office.

After they'd left, Dad looked at Matt and me. "Is there anything you need to talk to me about?" Our silence was his answer. "Good, let's hope the rest of the day is quieter."

After wading through the morning routine, Matt left for the autopsy. I touched base with Pete, who was dealing with several unrelated cases. He was very glad that we had excluded him from the morning visit from the Valkyrie.

I called Eddie and was surprised when he answered on the second ring. "Caller ID not working?" I asked.

"Hey, I'm not trying to avoid you." *Not right now*, I thought. "I got something for you. I don't want to talk about it on the phone."

"I'll meet you in Rose Hill at the north wall," I offered.

He considered it for a moment and agreed.

Rose Hill was the second oldest cemetery in Adams County. It was started in 1840 during an outbreak of yellow fever. Against the north wall were the graves of Union soldiers killed during the Civil War. The joke was that it was as far north as they could bury them and still be in the cemetery. There were over a hundred of the two-foot-high, rounded white gravestones with the name, rank and military unit of the deceased on them. I walked among them, wondering what it must have been like to die in a land both familiar yet foreign. I was glad that the wall blocked the cold north wind.

I saw Eddie looking furtive as he walked toward me, hunched over with his head covered by a hoodie. He looked up once in a while to make sure he was on course and to look right and left, just to make sure that anyone who saw him would be suspicious.

"Why don't you just shout 'I'm guilty of something' every couple of minutes," I asked.

He looked a little chagrined, but said, "This is dangerous.

My family gets wind of what I'm doing, I'm dead. Period. End of story." Actually, I believed him. Even a lot of the Thompsons that led relatively normal lives were a little scary.

"What have you got for me?" I didn't like any of this. It felt dirty, and I wanted to get it over with.

"There are a couple guys running molly in the county." Molly was the new meth, which was the new crack. Of course molly was already being replaced by flakka and whatever else someone wanted to use to get high. I hated dealing with drugs. Every time I heard about them, there was some new level that people were willing to go to to drop out. Just like the sixties—it was all about dropping out, only the music wasn't as good and the drugs were more toxic.

"Cut the bullshit. I want something related to my cases or the dirty cops you promised."

"I can't just tell people to hurry up and spill their secrets because I've got a deputy that's on a damn time schedule."

This is the point where I could have thrown him up against the wall and read him the riot act. But I didn't work that way, and I'd never been convinced that it was the best way to get the world to do your bidding.

"I told you I'm not going to start talking about the bad cops until I'm sure you aren't going to screw me, and I'm ready to leave this shithole. If you get your guys to take out these drug dealers, it will help a lot."

"Help who?"

"Me. Who do you think? But you too. It will help me get back into my family's good graces."

"When you were selling me this unique relationship, you told me you heard things all the time."

"I might have exaggerated my standing within the family just a little. I was honest about them abusing me. Trouble is, a lot of that hasn't stopped. And I don't get invited to the house very much."

"So how is me going after some drug dealers going to help your situation?"

"One of my cousins is having trouble with these guys. I

said I'd see if I could get them off the street. I didn't tell him how."

"I'm not in vice. But the way I understand it, guys who deal drugs are pretty savvy. It's not easy to catch them with the goods. Or at least not enough of the goods to have them taken off the street for any length of time." All I could think of was what a waste of time this was. Was he telling the truth about the crooked cops? I just couldn't be sure. I was beginning to think that this was turning into a Tar Baby situation.

"My cousin is close enough to them that he'll know when they have a full house. They aren't high-level guys. They deal with most of the shit themselves. Only thing they farm out is the street selling. Got kids doing that."

"Okay, what the hell, give me the details." I took it all down. He stiffed me for forty bucks to buy a burner phone to use to call me when it was time to have our men make a move on the dealers.

I left with him giving me assurances that this would give him the street cred he needed to be brought into his family's inner circle again. *What am I getting into?* was the only thing running through my mind as I drove away.

CHAPTER FOURTEEN

I called Dad to find out the time for Mauser's appointment.

"Three o'clock. I told his sitter to expect you," Dad said and hung up without more ado. It didn't sound like his day had improved much from the morning.

It was just noon, so I drove back to the office. There was no new information from forensics. I thought about calling, but I was always very cautious about nagging them. I'd heard enough rumors about what they would do if they decided they didn't like you. Their work-loads were so heavy that they were forced to prioritize. This meant that they had a choice—they could move your lab work to the top or the bottom of the pile depending on a varying set of circumstances, which included whether or not they liked you.

Matt was still at the autopsy and Pete was busy with cases. I went through my emails—nothing interesting there—and met with our direct supervisor, Lt. Johnson. On high-profile cases the chain of command was almost always superseded by the sheriff, but Johnson still needed to be kept in the loop. He was an Army man. Most of the guys in the department were pretty relaxed, but not Johnson. He always left you thinking you should have saluted him. After he heard about the fracas that morning, he looked positively relieved that Dad was taking personal supervision of the case.

I picked Mauser up without incident. The limp almost wasn't noticeable, but I was determined to have another meeting with Cara, the vet tech.

When we got to the vet, Mauser, the contrary beast that he was, hopped out of the van and headed straight to the door with only a minor detour to sniff the yard and to leave peemail for the other dogs. I had hoped he'd put up his usual temper tantrum so I could ask for Cara's help, but Mauser appeared to have his own agenda. We scared the crap out of a puppy being led out of the office by a proud new owner. Then I had to answer all of the owner's questions about Mauser while the puppy got brave enough to come over and sniff Mauser's shins. Having answered every repetitive Great Dane question there is, including *Have you got a saddle for him?* we finally got into the vet's.

Once inside, I began to worry that it might be Cara's day off. All kinds of worst-case scenarios ran through my mind as we sat on the wooden bench and waited. What if she'd been fired, or quit? But no worries. Ten minutes after three Cara came out of the back.

"There he is!" she said, her voice rising in excitement. I pretended that she was talking about me.

Mauser dragged me over to her, making it impossible for me to act suave or debonair. She patted his head as he smiled stupidly. Of course I was smiling stupidly too.

"Hi, it's nice to see you again," I said, wondering if the glamorous aura of Mauser would totally obscure me.

"Thanks, you too," she said, kneeling down and ruffling Mauser's ears and making eye contact with him as she spoke. *She* is *a vet tech*, I told myself.

"Your paw doesn't seem too bad," she chatted to him as we went into the back. Mauser and I were shown into an exam room without me getting a good opportunity to ask Cara out again.

"Why would she change her mind?" I asked Mauser

while we waited for the vet. The Dane raised his eyebrows and gave me a look that suggested my problems were of no concern to him. He turned around and presented his butt for me to scratch.

"You're a lot of support."

The doc came in and examined Mauser with the end result being that he didn't see anything wrong with the paw and that Dad should just keep an eye on it for a few days. Typical Dane drama.

We were headed for the front desk to check-out and I hadn't seen Cara again. I was kicking myself for not saying more to her when we got there. Then she appeared from the back, carrying his chart, which she gave to the receptionist.

Girding up my loins, whatever that means, I turned to Cara and, for once, she was looking at me and not Mauser.

"Would you walk out with us?" I asked.

She thought about it for second. "Sure, I don't mind spending a few more minutes with the big guy." Mauser leaned into her as she scratched his side. The receptionist said she'd bill Dad, and we headed for the door.

My pulse was racing as I thought about having my ego slammed into the pavement and stepped on again. But I was determined to take the chance. "I know you turned me down last time, but I thought maybe dinner sometime?" *Lamest move ever!* I thought.

"Actually... I've been in a kinda-sorta relationship with a guy." *That's it. Shot down again.* "But I finally broke it off with him this weekend. So... Sure, we could have dinner sometime."

I had a hard time understanding that she'd said yes. I almost asked her to repeat it, but I caught myself in time. Now I had to reorganize my thinking and come up with a response to yes.

"Ummm, great, how about tomorrow?" *Too soon. You've blown it again,* my inner self-hater said.

"Tomorrow? Sure, that'll work."

I was suddenly infused with adrenaline. With shaking

fingers, I entered her number in my phone's contact list and we agreed I'd pick her up Thursday at seven.

In the van headed back to Dad's, I turned to Mauser. "Oh shit, now I have a date. What the hell am I going to do?" His panting looked an awful lot like laughing from where I was sitting.

Once I was home, Ivy was no more sympathetic to my plight than Mauser. I fed her and grabbed dinner for myself. Then, when I should have been thinking about the murders, I was instead engrossed in plans for Thursday night. Where to go, what to wear and, lastly, what a fool I was. I texted Cara and asked if she'd like to go to Bella Bella, a romantic Italian restaurant in Tallahassee, even though I hated the idea of the long drive. It's hard to have your first real conversation with a date when you're driving, but you don't want to sit there in silence either. I just hoped we didn't end up spending the first half hour talking about Mauser.

Thursday morning was bright and cool as I drove to the office. Once there I found more lab reports on Mark Kemper waiting for me. Bloodwork showed no alcohol or other common drugs in his system. He was in reasonable health. Nothing to point in a different direction than where we were headed.

I caught up with Matt and got the low-down on Dell's autopsy. Again nothing to point us in a new direction. Comparing the damage to Kemper's face and Dell's left Dr. Darzi ninety-five percent sure that a different object was used in the two killings. We'd searched a mile around the area where Mark's body was found, all of the property around the warehouse and all that surrounded the motel and hadn't come up with any blunt objects that could have caused the injuries on either body. Our killer was either hanging onto the weapons or he'd been able to dispose of them somewhere we hadn't been able to find them.

Hair and fiber had been collected from both bodies and

crime scenes, but that wasn't much good without something to compare them to. Nothing odd or rare had been found that would be a smoking gun leading us to the perpetrator. Matt was still determined to find something in the evidence that would lead us to a suspect, but he was now more willing to give credence to my approach of motive first.

I talked to the Kempers again. They were flying back to Texas with their son's body the next day, but they were willing to come back for one more interview that afternoon.

Pete had found another person in the neighborhood who remembered the Danielses and would be willing to talk about them. I decided to re-interview Dad and see if I could get him to remember anything new about the different relationships within the group that he hung with.

Dad surprised me by sitting next to me in one of the leather wingback chairs instead of behind his mammoth desk as we walked through everything one more time.

"I've been trying to remember what all happened during the spring of that year. Because it really was just a couple of months that Mark Kemper was there when we were. He'd sort of hooked up with us after Christmas break. I think he was in study hall with Marget. He was pretty smart. Hung on Margret's every word. I think I felt sorry for him. He was too mature for the kids that were his age and, of course, a little too young to be hanging out with us. I don't think he was gay back then."

"Actually, I'm pretty sure that's not how it works."

"You know what I mean. He wasn't out or even very... ah... feminine. Just dressed a little too nice. And seemed more at home hanging out with the girls than with the guys. But at the time I probably just thought he was sweet on them."

"Nothing else?"

"Really, no. I went through a couple more yearbooks and there weren't a lot of other kids that hung around the house. That neighborhood was isolated back in those days. People pretty much hung with the kids that lived around them. You know I was over there a lot because Gramps had a big piece of his land up against the neighborhood. I had to help him out after school some. And once I noticed the girls, there was another reason to hang out at the Daniels house. Don't look at me like that. I was just a normal, red-blooded male. Nothing wrong with wanting to be around pretty girls."

An hour later I was sitting down with the Kempers. Grief had not brought them closer together. Mrs. Kemper asked if they could talk to me separately. I took her into the conference room where I'd talked to Dell and I left Mr. Kemper staring at the walls in the hallway.

"Did the coroner's office help you with the arrangements?"

"Arrangements is a funny word," was all she said.

"I know your loss must be unbearable."

"Do you? Mark was really the only thing in my life that meant anything. It was such a shock when he told us he was gay. It took me a year to accept what he was saying. But, gradually, I realized that he was my boy. He'd always be my son. And I wanted to be a part of his life and to love him for who he was. I know now that it was a great act of faith and love for him to tell me that he was gay. 'Cause he loved me too. And he was betting on me being a good mother. The type of mother who doesn't abandon her children because they are different."

I knew that she needed to talk, so I let her keep going. I couldn't imagine how alone she must have felt being with her husband who was cold as ice and hard as granite.

"Bill," she spat his name, "he could never bend. Never give an inch. God help me, I hate him. I thought he'd come around someday. Not him. Now there's no more somedays." She trailed off.

"Mrs. Kemper, we are going to do everything we can to catch his killer. We think this person killed someone else on Monday night."

This surprised her and she looked straight at me for the first time. "This Monday night? Who?"

"A woman named Dell McDonnell. Her maiden name was Daniels."

"Dell Daniels," she said thoughtfully. "Something…"

"She used to live here. In fact, in the same neighborhood as your family did." I didn't want to give her too much information. The idea was to learn what she knew. Anything I told her, she might incorporate as part of her memories.

"Yes, there was a Daniels family… They lived a street over from us."

"That's right."

"Mark was friends with their girls. I can't quite remember their names. But Dell sounds right. The other was Maggie or Marge… no, Margret, that's right. I didn't like her very much."

That was interesting. "Why didn't you like her?"

"I don't know. Well, that's not true, now that I think about it. She was mean to Mark."

"How was she mean to him?"

"He really liked her. Funny now that I think about it. I thought he was… you know… interested in her. He must have just liked her. But she treated him like dirt." I could see that it still made her mad to think about. "Marget'd make a date with him and be an hour late or not show up at all. Poor Mark would be so hurt. He'd mope about for hours or even days. I don't know what he saw in her. One time he saved up money from a small job he had at a garage detailing cars to buy her a birthday present. He came home from her party and cried for an hour. She'd told him that the pendant and earrings were junk jewelry. I almost went over there and said something, but he begged me not to. Then, all of a sudden, he didn't want to see her anymore."

"When was that?"

"This was sooo long ago. I guess his 'crush' went on for almost a year. So it would have been his sophomore year in high school."

"Did he tell you why he stopped seeing her?"

"I figured he got tired of the abuse. But I never thought about it much. I was just glad that he'd stopped going around that horrible girl. But you said it was her sister that got killed?"

"That's right. It was Dell, not Margret. Margret is still very much alive and I can tell you she hasn't improved with age." The last part almost got a smile from Mary.

"I don't really remember Dell. I guess she was around, and Mark might have talked about her. But I can't remember anything about her."

After a few more questions I escorted her out and ushered Bill Kemper in. He remembered less than his wife, but he had a slightly different take on Margret.

"I was happy that he'd found a girl. I guess I already sensed that there was something wrong with Mark."

I wanted to correct him on the part about *something wrong*, but I needed to keep the interview focused on getting as much information as possible. "Did you meet her?"

"Yeah, I did. She was quite a package. I was really proud of the boy for getting a pretty girl like that to go out with him. Of course things didn't go very smoothly. Guess we now know why. Shame, I thought she might make a man out of him. I swear they were pretty close. He let me down. Dropping her was a big mistake. That's pretty much when everything started going to shit."

"What do you mean?"

"His grades and everything started going downhill after they broke up. At first I thought it was just the usual 'Dear John' blues, but they never picked up again. Stopped playing baseball, grades went from A's to C's. Never failed anything, but never reached his potential. Must have found out he was queer. That'd mess you up for sure."

I was about done listening to this homophobe. I asked a few more general questions, then escorted both the Kempers outside.

I held the door for Mrs. Kemper. She turned to me and

handed me a card with a number on it. "That's my cell phone number; you can reach me there anytime. Don't bother calling the house. I won't be there."

"I'll call. Good luck," I told her.

Heading back to my desk, I looked at my watch and realized I needed to finish up and get out of there if I was going to be ready for my date with Cara.

CHAPTER FIFTEEN

I drove slowly down the street, looking for Cara's duplex. It was a cute little brick house that looked like it had been meant as a duplex rather than converted later. I double-checked to make sure I had the right address before knocking.

"Be right there." When the door opened, Cara pushed a small black nose back from the door and asked me in.

Cara looked beautiful in a green sweater and black jeans. I realized I'd never seen her wearing anything but vet tech scrubs. Staring at me from the floor was a stout little Pug giving me the once over. He moved forward and sniffed my legs, then backed up again and resumed staring up at me.

"This is Alvin. He was abandoned at the vet with a thousand-dollar bill for a broken leg."

"I hope you got a discount."

"I did, but he'd have been worth it either way. Besides being the perfect roommate, he has impeccable taste in men. If I had listened to him when he barked at the last guy, I could have saved myself six months with a jerk."

"Do you think I pass the test?" Alvin and I stared at one another.

"At least he's not barking." She smiled.

Once in the car I was determined to keep the conversation light and airy.

"You're a cop?" was her first question.

"Yeah, sort of. I'm a deputy with the sheriff's department."

"Is there a difference?"

"Yeah. Well… cops work for cities. Deputies work for the sheriff." I didn't think this was a great way to start a romantic evening.

"Oh, okay. But they pretty much do the same thing?"

"Yeah, pretty much." Round one to Cara.

Should I turn on music? No, then I'd have to decide on what type of music. "Where are you from?" I decided to go with a simple question.

"Wherever I am," she said, laughing lightly. *That's the sort of answer a crazy person gives*, I thought.

"Do you carry a gun?" she asked next. *What the hell? That's the next question a crazy person would ask*, my mind screamed. "I haven't been around guns much," she added. *Probably a good thing*, my inner voice responded.

This wasn't going very well. I had no idea what to say. I had a beautiful woman in my car, but she seemed to be determined to put me on the defensive.

"Your father's the sheriff. How'd that happen?" *What kind of question was that?*

"He ran for office almost eight years ago and won. He's never had a serious challenger since." I glanced over and she was nodding her head.

"So you work for your dad?" Her voice was light, but it was hard not to hear the question as an accusation.

"I'm sorry if you have a problem with my job." If the idea was to put me on the defensive, she'd succeeded.

"No, not really. I just never went out with a cop." *Deputy, I'm a deputy*, I wanted to scream. Fifteen minutes into the date and I wasn't sure that I could get through it with my sanity intact.

"I don't really like being a deputy, if that makes you feel

any better," I said.

"That's interesting. You can't find other work?"

"I'm pretty sure I could find something else to do. I just… I… It's hard to explain."

"I don't mind listening."

Oh, God, should I really go into all of it? At this point, what do I have to lose? "Okay, but the story is long and probably not that interesting to anyone who isn't me." I sighed, glancing over to see her looking at me with interest.

"I was almost finished with my second year of college—this was ten years ago—and my mom suffered an aneurysm. It was sudden, no indications of any kind. One minute she was walking from the kitchen to the living room and the next second she was lying on the floor. Dad was right there. The ambulance showed up in ten minutes. She was at the hospital forty minutes after she hit the floor, but she never regained consciousness. I came home as soon as Dad called me. For almost a month we sat by her bedside. Dad grabbed for every shred of hope he could find. Nothing. For all practical purposes, she was dead before the ambulance arrived. We faced the reality only when we had no choice. Taking her off of life support nearly killed my dad. He could accept that she couldn't live, but to have to make the decision that led to her passing from this world was almost too much for him.

"I couldn't go back to school. At least not until I saw my dad through the grief. I'm the one that suggested he run for sheriff. I said it because Mom had always kidded him about running. It was a regular joke. When she wanted to get him out of a grumpy mood she'd call him Sheriff Macklin and it always made him smile. He'd risen to captain within the department and the current sheriff was retiring. So I told him that Mom would find it the perfect joke if he ran for sheriff. I didn't think he'd do it. Then one day he looked at me and said, 'I bet it *would* make her smile.' But he said if he ran he wanted me to join the department as a deputy. I told him that if he'd take his campaign for sheriff seriously, then

I'd go to the academy. He won and I became a deputy."

"That's actually a beautiful story," Cara said.

We were almost to Tallahassee. I wondered what had just happened. I hadn't ever told anyone that story. Our friends knew parts of it, but I'd never told anyone the whole thing. I looked over at Cara. She was humming softly to herself. *She might really be a witch*, I thought with a smile.

Stepping out of the car, the cool crisp autumn air felt refreshing. I touched her hand and she let me take it in mine.

While we waited for our food, I was determined to learn something about this interesting nymph. After the waiter brought our wine, I said, "You were a bit evasive when I asked where you're from."

"Is this the way you interrogate suspects?" she asked, but smiled sweetly. "Okay, I'll confess. I was born in a car somewhere in Louisiana. My parents were never real clear on where. Honestly, my parents are seldom clear on anything. The first real home I remember was in Kentucky. My father worked for a horse farm until he learned what they did to the horses to make them race, even if they weren't physically fit to run. But we stayed in Kentucky for a while. Dad went to work for some guys who thought they could build a sustainable community in the hill country. It worked for a while, but my parents were the only ones who took it seriously. Everyone else just used it as a place to crash while scoring whatever drugs they could find. We left and headed down here to Gainesville. That hippy town was made for my parents. Mom grows and sells herbs. Dad taught gardening, animal husbandry and blacksmithing when we first moved there. Now he manages the co-op they live in. I came up here five years ago because I needed a little space from them." She leaned forward. "You're good. You got my whole life history in five minutes."

"I thought we'd be talking about what bands we like or which movies are the best," I said after the waiter brought our food.

"I couldn't care less what bands a guy likes. I want to

know who he is. Tastes change, the fundamentals of character don't," she said just before diving into her eggplant rollatini. I started on my capellini marinara. The food was excellent and we ate in companionable silence.

Full and feeling more relaxed, we waited for the check.

"Are you working on a case?"

"I'm always working on a case. Several right now."

"Anything you can tell me about them?" Cara took the last swallow of wine from her glass.

"Just the details that our press officer has made public. But I'm surprised that you're interested."

"You think because my family is full-on hippy that we aren't tough? That would be a mistake. We saw the dark side more than once when we were on the road. Mom and Dad taught me to look at life the way it is, but to try and make it the way it should be." She said this last with a sincerity and sadness that spoke of someone who's seen some bad things.

"I'm working on two murder cases and an arson." I couldn't tell her that they were related. The department was still holding that information back. I gave her a few more details that had been in the paper and she listened with interest.

On the way home we talked about Mauser, Alvin and Ivy… the really important things in life. Too soon, I pulled up to her duplex.

"No invite to go over to your house or a request to come in for a nightcap?"

"Does anyone say 'nightcap' anymore?" I asked her.

"I just did, but I have a bad habit of watching old movies before I go to bed." The wine had made her voice higher and the giggles more regular.

"I *am* going to walk you to your door," I said. "But I figure I'll either get a second date and we'll see where we go then, or this is the last date we're going to have and, if that's the case, what are the odds you're going to invite me in? I can save myself the humiliation."

"Second date, then. And this time I get to name the time

and place."

"Fair enough." I turned serious. "I *have* enjoyed it."

I got out of the car and came around to open her door, but she was waiting for me by the time I got to her side. We walked to the house and she unlocked the door, turning back to me. I leaned in and she moved her lips to meet mine. They touched for a moment before parting.

"Good night," we said together.

I bounced back to the car. Not love, not yet. But affection for sure, and just being "in affection" with someone felt new and fresh.

My phone started ringing as I got to the car. I looked to see who it was before I answered.

"What is it, Eddie?" I asked, plummeting back to earth at the sight of his name.

"Tomorrow. Early afternoon."

"What? Do you mean it's time to move in on the dealers?"

"Tomorrow's Friday. They always try to have a lot on hand for Friday afternoon 'cause people get paid and are buying for the weekend."

"This better go down easy." *Jesus, I'm doing the cops and robbers thing again.* "If this is some kind of trick, I will find you and beat your ass." I meant it.

"You hit them at the house around noon, you'll make a haul. I'm serious." Did he have to add the *I'm serious*? That just made me skeptical.

"How well armed are these guys?"

"They've always got guns, but they don't know shit about them. I doubt they've ever done more than shoot them up in the air."

Eddie gave me the address of the drug den. "You have this phone with you tomorrow. Understand?"

"Yeah, no problem."

"I'll talk to you when it's done." I hung up, frustrated. I had wanted to indulge in thoughts of Cara and our evening together, but now my mind was filled with all the crap I needed to do to get ready for tomorrow. Plus, there were all the things that could go wrong and the consequences if they did.

By eleven o'clock Friday the squad that would enter the house was suited up. The warrant had been granted based on my confidential informant's statements and several complaints that I found from neighbors about activity at the residence. It was a "no-knock" warrant, which I was morally opposed to, but I'd checked and double-checked the address and had driven by it first thing that morning, just to be sure.

The squad was made up of half a dozen deputies that served as our SWAT team when they weren't doing road duty. We also had a DEA agent from Tallahassee. I felt awkward and out of place wearing body armor. I'd turned down the M16 they'd offered me. I'd qualified on one, but I felt more comfortable with my Glock handgun. I'd brought two extra magazines and had checked all three twice and made sure that I had a round in the chamber.

The sergeant leading the SWAT team would direct the entry and I would be in charge of the scene and the suspects once the building was secured. We got ready to move and everyone stood poised, waiting for my watch to tell us to converge on the location. I thought about calling Eddie one more time, but didn't. Eleven-fifty. I keyed my radio.

"Go."

Twenty minutes later I was looking at a couple of knuckleheads lying on the floor, hands cuffed behind their backs, whining about lawyers and rights. The DEA agent was using his flashlight to look at the drugs lying everywhere around the house. The windows were all covered to keep out prying eyes and the lamps must have had forty-watt blubs in them. *Were they trying to save money?* I thought. Maybe the low light was better when all your clients had dilated eyes.

"Lot of shit here," the agent said happily. "Enough to put these scumbags away for a long time." He thumped one of them with a large black boot.

"Plenty of guns too," the SWAT leader said, looking in a closet.

So a happy ending. But I wasn't sure. Something about this bothered me. Maybe it was too easy. You get some information, you raid a house and, boom, you have a big collar. Maybe I didn't like it because I knew that I was doing the dirty work for other dealers. But I couldn't let it bother me now. The deal had been made. I went outside and called Eddie.

"Told you," he said as soon as he answered. I looked around. He must have seen it go down or had someone else watching. Most likely the former. He wouldn't want anyone else knowing what he was doing. *Unless he's not the one directing this and you are totally being played*, said the negative nelly voice in my head.

"Good so far, my cross-dressing confidential informant. But there better be more to come."

"I'm delivering."

"And I delivered for you. But this was just the first step in our partnership, right?"

"I said so. Man, you are hard. What the hell is it going to take for you to trust me?"

"That probably isn't ever going to happen, so let's just work on our little joint project one step at a time, never forgetting that we are working toward an ultimate end. Okay?"

"I'm on your side, man." He sounded wounded.

Feeling like a sucker, I told him, "Thank you. You were spot-on with this bust. Call me if there's anything I need to know."

"Okay. Bye."

I hadn't realized that having a CI was going to involve the same ups and downs as maintaining a romantic relationship.

As I headed back toward the house, my phone rang. I looked at the name: Kemper—Frye. I had a system for keeping track of witnesses and other interested parties. When I put someone connected with a case into my contacts list, I put the name of the case first, then the last name of the person and sometimes a first initial. So I knew that this was Mark Kemper's ex-boyfriend calling.

"Mr. Frye, what can I do for you?"

"I was looking over the texts I got from Mark over the last couple of months. And there were some funny ones." His voice trailed off. His words were a little slurred. At noon? On a weekday? Killers destroy so many lives.

"What do you mean by funny?"

"Okay, one says, and I quote: 'I'm thinking of doing something I should have done a long time ago.'"

"Did you ask him what he meant?"

"Of course. He said: 'You wouldn't understand.' No wait. It says 'couldn't understand.'"

"Do you have any idea what he meant?"

"No, and I just let it go at the time. We used to get in arguments about how I didn't understand how he felt, and he couldn't understand what I was going through… All that crazy shit you say when you're arguing with someone you love." I could hear him choking up. "Oh, hell."

"Were there any more?" I felt bad for him, but keeping him focused might be the best way to get both of us through this call.

"A couple. Just a week ago he sent one that said: 'I'm going home. Hope you don't hate me when you find out why.' I told him I didn't know what he was talking about. And he said, and I quote: 'You'll know soon enough. Wish me luck.'"

"Did you call him or email him and ask more questions?"

"No. Look, you had to know Mark. He was funny and sweet, but he could also be very melodramatic sometimes. I tried not to feed into it. Wait, there was one more I missed earlier. He said: 'Don't worry, it's just family business.' Which means nothing to me. His mom is just about the only family he had. A few cousins that live out on the west coast, but they're on his father's side and... Well, screw that old man."

"Can you think of anything else that might help?"

"Nothing can help at this point. It's all turned to shit. I guess Mark wasn't the only one that could be melodramatic, huh?"

"You've suffered a horrible loss. Talk to someone. Family. A professional. A friend."

"I talked to Mark's mom last night. I feel so bad for her. I think I'm going to go visit her. She's going to have a memorial for Mark. She asked me to stay with her."

"She seemed like a nice woman."

"Mark loved her. He would have loved that asshole father of his if that toad would have given him a chance. Mark said once that he thought fathers should be forgiven. That it could be hard to know what the right thing to do was." His voice just trailed off.

"Thanks for calling. If you think of anything or need anything, call me."

"Sure. I'm going to go get royally messed up now. Bye."

I looked up to see the DEA agent standing there. My sympathy for Frye must have shown on my face. "Are you all right?" he asked.

I shook my head. "How's it looking?"

"We're tagging and bagging now. All of it will go through your evidence room. The only thing that we need is to check all the electronic devices to see if any of them can give us some intel on operations up the food chain. Of course, anything that is local we'll share with your department..."

He went on, but I lost track of the conversation. Officers who specialize in a certain area get tunnel vision that sometimes prevents them from seeing the world around them. Everything has to revolve around drugs or guns or SWAT operations. I could never see life through that narrow of a lens.

CHAPTER SIXTEEN

We spent the rest of the day cleaning the house out, interviewing the suspects—which included recording gems such as: "It's my cousin's house, man" and "We was just fooling around"—and then finally writing up the reports.

At seven o'clock my phone rang... Dad's gunshots.

"Nice job!" High praise from the parental unit.

"Thanks," I said, exhausted.

"I have a couple news crews coming into the office for an interview. Meet us in the large conference room in half an hour." He hung up. Guess it wasn't optional.

With video rolling and cameras clicking, the DEA agent talked about the amount and value of all the drugs. Dad gave them the standard stump speech about the need to be ever-vigilant in keeping our county clean. We all stood behind a table where a large sample of the drugs and guns was laid out. Dad even shook my hand for the cameras. Why didn't it feel better? Was it because it was a gift that I was going to have to pay for later? Maybe. Or maybe drugs always left me feeling dirty. At last the news people left and I was finally free to go home.

After a shower, food and time with Ivy, I had a moment to think about the murders. I'd been the lead on five homicides since I became an investigator. The first one was vehicular. We found the driver within twelve hours. She'd been drunk and her significant other called us when he found the car in the garage, bloody and damaged. The second was a body dump by drug dealers. It took a week, but one of them told a friend who told a friend who dropped a dime on them to get off of a possession charge. The third was a body found in the woods, decayed and unidentifiable. She was still on our books as a Jane Doe. Possibly sexual assault, maybe a serial killer. I came back to it when I had some time.

The fourth was a real TV whodunit. Woman found in her bathtub, husband claimed she had committed suicide by pills. The coroner said that the marks on her body indicated she'd been held underwater and that the pills she'd taken were not fully digested and therefore hadn't had time to enter her system. The husband was still awaiting trial.

The fifth and last was a barbecue shoot-out. A family having a cookout when friends of one guy got in an argument with friends of another guy. Knives and guns came out. Three people injured and one man dead. Two days of taking statements finally got us to some version of the truth and a charge of second-degree manslaughter.

Now I had a real puzzler. Two murders, one arson and no physical evidence tying them together. Not that we didn't *have* any physical evidence. In fact, a ton of trace evidence was collected at both the Kemper dumpsite and the murder and dismemberment site. But it would be months before most of it was processed. Fibers, hair and possible DNA samples were found at the second murder site as well, but since it was a motel room, God knows how many people left evidence in that room. It looked like our killer was only there for a short time. If he or she left anything, it was mixed up with dozens of other samples. Again, it would be months before it was analyzed. We might eventually get enough evidence to convict, but not to discover.

That meant we had to find the motive. I had already

decided to give up my Saturday and go over to the Danielses neighborhood and question the old timer that Pete had identified. Something that happened back then had to hold the answer. But what? Something in the text that Mark had sent his boyfriend was nagging at me. I texted Frye and asked him to copy them to an email and send it to me. After I looked over them, I might want to call Mrs. Kemper and talk with her again.

Pete met me at the office the next morning. The place was quiet on Saturday.

"You don't have to go out there with me," I told him.

"Are you kidding? Sarah is already getting ready for Thanksgiving. She's driving me crazy. I would have paid money to come into work today." He squeezed into my car and put his sixty-four ounce Coke in the cup holder. "The guy's name is Leonard Watkins. Lives two doors down from the Daniels house."

It had turned warm again. That was life in north Florida. These days the seasons seemed to intermingle. All except summer. Summer was just plain hot.

Mr. Watkins's yard was immaculate. There wasn't a lot of landscaping, but what was there was trimmed and mowed to within an inch of its life. Before we reached the front door the garage opened. A tall black man with greying hair stood there holding a large piece of wood.

"Heard you drive up." He held up the piece of wood. "Working on a bench for the backyard." He put the wood down. "Come on through."

We followed him through an OCD workshop. There were hospital operating rooms dirtier than his garage. We entered an equally well maintained backyard where we took seats around a glass-topped table.

"Deputy Henley here," he indicated Pete, "said you all were investigating the fire at the Daniels house. He said you all thought it might have something to do with the kids that used to hang out there."

"That's right. You were living here then?"

"We were the second black family to move into the neighborhood. We moved here in 1977. The Echols were the first. They moved here in '75. They took most of the crap for being the first. Us, not too much. There was a cross on our lawn, but the morons never got it lit. Our mailbox was smashed a couple times, but that might have just been kids doing stupid shit, because a couple white neighbors' boxes were vandalized too. Hell, the cross turned out to be a good thing. My wife was freaking before that because no one was talking to us, but after that several of the families, including the Danielses, came over and told us that that wasn't what the neighborhood was all about. Mr. Daniels and Tom Canfield offered to stand watch and make sure it didn't happen again. Broke the ice."

"So you knew the Daniels family pretty well?"

"I wouldn't say that. We got invited to some backyard cookouts and a few Christmas parties. I knew everyone in the family by sight. We waved to each other." He shrugged.

I gave Pete the *What are we doing here?* look. He stepped in. "You knew Mark Kemper pretty well," Pete said to Mr. Watkins.

"Yeah, I knew Mark real well. Super nice kid. I can't believe he was killed." He shook his head. "At first he kind of stopped by like everyone else after the cross. Told me how bad he felt. But then he just kept coming by. He'd help me with building projects or work in the yard, that kind of stuff. He kept in touch after he moved away too. When I found out he was gay it kind of all made sense."

Mr. Watkins saw my raised eyebrows. "No, no, man, nothing like that. I just think he saw us as outsiders too. You know. He felt different and here was this family in the neighborhood who were different too. Also, it was the seventies. I was young, into the funky scene a little. I'd dress to the nines when I wanted to and play some serious R&B. I gave him some tapes. Different times, man."

"Did he tell you about any problems or concerns he had?"

"I've been trying to think of anything that might help. Though I can't see how anything back then could have caused someone to kill him today. Hey, wait, I did dig up something." He got up and headed to the house. "You want anything to drink?" Pete and I declined the offer.

A few minutes later he came back carrying an old photo album. He put it on the table, opened to a page with half a dozen photos. Most of the pictures featured various people posed around Leonard and a bright yellow Trans-Am.

"I loved that car. Wish I still had it." He pointed at a picture of himself and a young man with long, light-colored hair wearing cut-off blue jeans and a plaid shirt. "That's Mark. I let him borrow the car a few times." He shook his head. "That's how trustworthy he was. I can't imagine letting some sixteen-year-old borrow my car today. Let alone a car like that. But the times he took it out, it came back with a full tank and clean as a whistle."

"Why'd he borrow the car?"

"Ha, why do you think a teenager wants to borrow a hot car? He had a date, man. Of course, that's kinda funny now. But I guess he was still trying to find himself back then."

"Was it one of the Daniels girls?" I asked.

He got a thoughtful look on his face. "I think so." He turned the page in the album and pointed to another picture of Mark and the car. In this picture, taken at night, there was a girl sitting in the passenger seat. The glare from the flash reflecting off of the window made it hard to make out her details. It could have been one of the Daniels girls, or maybe not.

"Do you remember anything odd or out of place?"

"I always thought it was funny that after that first year he never asked to borrow the car again. A couple times I made jokes about it being Saturday night and didn't he need the car for a hot date? He'd just shake his head and say he didn't have a date. I guess he tried the dating a girl thing, then realized that wasn't his way. Tough road to go in those days."

"Would your wife remember anything from those days?"

"Ex-wife. No, I doubt it. She hated the neighborhood. Her family all lived down in Creekton. She wanted us to live down there too. After we moved here she still spent all of her free time down there with her family." He pointed to the car again. "Absolutely hated that car. When we got divorced, I think the only thing she really wanted was to force me to sell it. Did too. Bitch." If his ex-wife was found dead, especially if she was run over by a Trans-Am, the prime suspect would be obvious.

We thanked him for his time and got up to go. Walking back through the garage, I remembered something. "You said that Mark kept in touch. When was the last time you heard from him?"

"You know, he messaged me on Facebook. Wait here." We waited by my car until Watkins came out to the driveway carrying an iPad.

"There." He handed me the tablet, pointing to the Facebook message from Mark. It said: *Might be down your way in a couple of months. Haven't decided.* I thanked Mr. Watkins for his time and we drove away.

"Not much in the message."

"No, but he was trying to make some decision. The texts he sent to his ex-boyfriend all point to that too. Something was eating at him."

Back at the office, I went to my desk to check emails. I found one from Frye. He'd included about fifty text messages that dated back six months. A lot of them were of the "wish you were here" variety. Only the last few seemed to indicate Mark had been grappling with some problem, a problem that involved him coming here. Then I saw what had been bothering me.

Pete had followed me back into the office, still unwilling to face his wife in the early stages of a holiday frenzy. "Hey, Pete, take a look at these. The last dozen in particular, and tell me what you think." He came around my desk and looked at the email.

"He was upset about something and he was going to come here and deal with it. What else?"

"This one." The text I pointed to said: *Don't worry, it's just family business.* "Frye read it to me when I talked to him on the phone, but it hadn't jumped out at me even though he seemed to think it was strange."

"Family business."

"Exactly. Whatever he had to do here, or wanted to do here, had to do with his family. I'm going to call Mrs. Kemper again. Maybe he had a cousin or someone who was 'like family' to him."

I picked up my phone and found the number listed as Kemper—Mom. She answered on the fourth ring.

"Yes?"

"Mrs. Kemper, this is Deputy Macklin. I hope you had a safe trip home."

"Yes, thank you." Her voice was flat and emotionless. Drugs. Do they still prescribe Valium?

"I'm sorry to bother you, but I had a couple questions I was hoping you could answer."

"Anything… Anything I can do to help."

"Did Mark have any family down here?"

"Family? No, all of our family is out here. Even then, there isn't much. Mark had some cousins on… his father's side. My sister passed away ten years ago. I still keep in touch with her husband, but I don't think Mark did. They never had children. My parents are both dead. Heart disease and cancer ran in both our families. I think that's partly why Mark did the work he did. Said he felt safer spending half his time in hospitals. He used to joke that if he had a heart attack on the job, a doctor wouldn't be far away."

"Do you know what he might have meant if he said he had some family business to take care of here?"

She was quiet for a while. "No, really, I can't imagine." The words just trailed away.

"Did Mr. Frye get ahold of you?" I felt like I needed to do something to help.

"He did. A very nice man. I wish I'd encouraged their relationship more."

"He seems lost without your son."

She started to speak and choked up. "He's coming to stay when we have the memorial. I'm looking forward to seeing him."

"I'm sorry I can't come to the service."

"Just find the person who did this and put them someplace far away from decent people so they can't hurt anyone else."

"I'm going to do my best," I said lamely. "I'll let you know when we make some progress."

"Thank you. Call anytime." She hung up.

I looked up to see Pete fuming at his phone. "Damn, why did I check my phone? I'd 'accidently' left it on vibrate. At least ten messages, most of them stuff I need to pick up. Shit." He got to his feet. "Better get going. Are the holidays over yet?"

"Haven't even started," I said, receiving an over-the-shoulder bird from him.

I looked at the clock. Past noon. I knew I shouldn't waste my whole Saturday at the office. The place was quiet, almost creepy, on the weekends when most of the administrative staff was off.

I walked into the main hallway, reading a text on my phone and not paying attention to my surroundings. At the academy they taught us we should have situational awareness at all times. Big fail. I was jumped and almost knocked to the floor. The hot fetid breath of my assailant smelled of hot dogs and ice cream. The attack was accompanied by a low and friendly bark.

Dad's voice shouted from his office, "Mauser, whatever you're doing, quit it!"

"He almost killed me. I think I peed my pants."

"Wouldn't be the first time," Dad shouted back. Mauser

chewed on my arm in greeting. I let him drag me into Dad's office. Mauser always liked to show off his captured prey. Finally I shook off the monster dog.

"What're you doing here on a Saturday?" Dad asked, barely looking up from his computer.

"It's either work the Kemper and McDonnell cases, or I could declare you the prime suspect, arrest you and call it a day," I said.

He looked up at me. "I wish I could remember something that could help."

"Kemper said that he was coming here because of family business. Does that mean anything to you?"

"I just didn't know the kid that well. You know how it is in high school. You may try to hang out with people who are older than you like he did, but you always avoid hanging out with the younger kids. I just ignored him. Probably hoped he'd go away. Maybe you should focus on Dell. I can't argue with your logic that the cases are connected, but it's odd because the way I remember it, Mark and Dell didn't have that much to do with each other. Dell might be the center pin instead of Kemper. It was her house that got burned."

"The killer is after Dell or something to do with Dell. Kemper finds out and confronts the killer and boom! Then the killer goes about his business burning down the house, which brings Dell to town, giving him the opportunity to kill her. That makes some sense, I guess." It made as much sense as anything else anyway.

"So why would someone want to kill the nicest woman anyone has ever met?" Mauser was bored by the whole work thing and sat down on my feet, leaning back against me. It's a Dane thing. "I guess I could talk to her sister again." I stopped, hoping Dad would talk me out of that crazy idea.

"Ha, good idea and good luck." He was trying to type emails as we talked.

"Yeah, I'll call Tim and see if he can be there to help control the harridan."

"I talked to him yesterday evening. They're thinking about turning off the life support on his father the first of the week. Might be best if you talk to them sooner rather than later."

"Thanks," I said sincerely. It's always best to know what you're walking into, and it would be better to talk to them before they had to deal with the funeral and whatever else. I shoved Mauser off of me. "Talk to you later."

He waved without looking up from his computer screen.

I headed out to my car. The air was warm with only a trace of fall. I rolled the windows down and dialed Tim's number. Pleasantries over, I told him I was hoping to talk to his mother and get some more background about his aunt.

"You really think this has something to do with Aunt Dell's past?" He sounded skeptical.

"We're looking into everything."

"Have you discovered any clues?"

Clues? Like this was a Scooby-Doo mystery. "We have some evidence, but no solid leads. It would be a big help if you could arrange for a sit-down with your mother. I know you have a lot on your mind right—"

"No, no, I can talk to her. But I can't promise anything. You never know what kind of mood she's going to be in."

"I can imagine. I'm free this afternoon."

"I'll check with her and see. She's staying here with me. I don't think Dad would approve, but, well, she's rather strong-minded."

"I did notice that," I said sympathetically.

"I'll call you back."

I felt sorry for the poor guy. He must have been going nuts, with his dad dying and his batshit crazy mother running around on the rampage because her sister was murdered.

I was almost home when my phone rang. "She said she'll meet you at three. Here at the main house." I looked at my watch. That gave me just enough time to have lunch and get there in plenty of time.

"I'll be there. Thanks."

I'd been out to the Devries farm several times with Dad. A large farmhouse sat in the middle of six hundred acres of prime hay fields. They owned another three thousand acres scattered around the county that they farmed and another two thousand they used for hunting. A dozen different houses dotted the various properties, some of them lived in by farm-hands while others were rented out. If the Devrieses weren't the wealthiest land owners in the county, it was only because some of our large hunting tracts were owned by rich folks from south and central Florida. But I'd never heard of the father or son being anything but humble, God-fearing country folk.

I turned at their gate and drove for ten more minutes before I saw the house. It was big, but not fancy. The yard was neat and well tended without a lot of ornamentation. The only thing that stood out was the Mercedes with Duval County tags parked out front.

I didn't have to knock. Tim opened the door as soon as I stepped onto the porch.

"Good to see you." He stepped out and shook my hand, then ushered me into the house.

The hallway was wide and ran from the front door to the back. The smell of polished wood and old rugs filled the air as I followed him into the first room on the right. It was a huge living room with heavy furniture that was built before Teddy Roosevelt charged up San Juan Hill.

Margret was seated on an overstuffed sofa, trying to look at home even though Jim had kicked her out a decade earlier, albeit with a golden parachute.

"I don't know what you think I can tell you," she said, already sounding bored.

"I appreciate you taking the time to see me," I said, trying to grease the wheels.

"Well…"

"Have a seat," Tim said, offering me several choices. I

took the wingback chair across from her royal highness of nothing.

"I can't imagine that there is anything else I can tell you."

"I've talked to a few people who knew you all back then. I might be able to help you remember some things that have slipped you mind."

She gave me a look of pure fire. "Go on." Her tone was icy.

"Several people said that you went out on some dates with Mark Kemper."

"Really? I guess it's possible. I can't say I remember that. But I was pretty damn good-looking back then. I went on a lot of dates." She was trying very hard to sound nonchalant about it, but I could tell she didn't like this at all. What was surprising was that she was willing to sit there and take it.

I had to phrase my questions so that they weren't too accusatory. I didn't want to push her over the edge and get shut down. "One guy told me that he lent Mark his yellow Trans-Am to go on a date with you."

"There you go! I probably went out with him because of the car. After all, Mark was gay. What difference does it make if I went out with him?" She laughed and looked around as if she expected everyone to find that amusing.

"I just want to know if you remember going out with him."

"But why? I guess I do, but what the hell difference does it make?"

She actually had me there. What difference *did* it make? "I am just looking at all the relationships from that time. Because that was the only time that your sister, your house and Mark all came in contact."

"Makes some sense, I guess. But I can't tell you anything that would help you find the killer. The killer is out there someplace." She waved her hand dramatically toward the windows. "Not hiding in the past."

"I think the question I want you to really think about is why would someone kill your sister and Mark Kemper? Can you think of anyone that was involved with both of them? Other than you, my father and Jim."

"No. I really can't. This is maddening because I know that this has nothing to do with us. The killer is probably a nut job who just happened to run into two people who knew each other a long time ago. Now I have to call an end to this unless you have something reasonable to ask, or some information that would help us to understand this tragedy."

I knew when I'd been beat. I stood up. "I can't tell you that I'm done asking you questions."

She gave me a smile and then turned to her son and said, "I'll be here if you need to talk to me again." A look passed between mother and son. I wasn't sure exactly what it was, but I knew it had nothing to do with maternal love. I don't think Tim was looking forward to having his mother under the same roof for an extended period.

Tim walked me to the door. "I really would like to help in any way I can. But, honestly, I don't think my mother knows or remembers anything from back then that could help. She pretty much lives in the here and now."

"Thanks. Oh, and Dad told me about your father. I'm sorry."

"I'm going to spend the next couple of days with him and then we'll have them remove life support. The doctors give him no chance of recovery and if he did wake up, he'd be severely brain-damaged. He never would have wanted that."

"Both my dad and I have living wills filled out for just that reason."

Tim gave a bitter laugh. "You know my dad. Everything was a handshake deal. He never felt like contracts and wills were necessary. Got us into trouble a couple of times. But that was Dad."

With nothing more I could say, I got in my car and drove off.

On the way home, I thought about Cara. Was she ever going to call me, or was that her way of ditching me? I doubted it. She was definitely a straight-forward, tell-it-like-it-is, kind of woman. Which is just the kind I like. If she didn't want to see me again, she'd have just said it right out.

After dinner, I spent time reviewing the files I'd brought home, looking through the crime scene photos and making notes, trying once again to understand the person who committed these murders. They were brutal crimes of passion. The only thing I managed to do was give myself nightmares.

CHAPTER SEVENTEEN

When I got up on Sunday, my plan was to give my mind a rest and forget about the cases. I did some work outside until one o'clock, when I got a call from Pete.

"Help."

"Pete?"

"I remembered that you needed to go out to the range today and practice for your qualifications," he said, which made no sense since we had both done our recertification just three months earlier.

"What are you talking about?" I asked, genuinely puzzled.

"Right, I know you need the practice. I told Sarah that I would help you out with some pointers," he went on.

Oh, I got it. Pete wanted to get out of the house and this was the best excuse he could come up with. Actually, banging away at some targets *did* sound like a good way to relax.

"Do you want me to pick you—" I didn't get a chance to finish.

"I'll head your way as soon as I pack my range bag. Yeah, I figured we'd be there a while." I guess he added that last bit for Sarah's benefit.

The sheriff's department shared a range with Calhoun's

police department. Now, mind you, they only had fifteen officers total so we ran the range and they just came out to use it. We had two private bays and one large open bay for group training. Pete drove us to the larger of the two individual bays.

"Seriously, you need to get married," Pete said, breathing heavily as he lugged gear to the shooting benches.

"Why?" I asked, lending a hand.

"Because I'm sick and tired of being the one who's begging his partner to help him escape."

"You love Sarah."

"True, that is very true. Loving someone does not mean that they can't drive you crazy and vice versa. When she's in one of these manic cleaning modes, I just want to go camp in the woods until it's over. Why the hell didn't my father take me hunting? That's what most of the guys do during the holidays."

"Did you bring enough guns?" I asked rhetorically, seeing the half dozen different weapons he was carting over to the bench.

"I plan on being out here until it's too dark to see the targets. Of course I've got a flashlight, so maybe a little later."

"It can't be that bad."

"The trouble is, her mother's coming for Thanksgiving. Sarah has this huge inferiority complex where her mother is concerned. And her mother doesn't help. The minute she walks in the house, she'll be looking for something to criticize about Sarah's housework. It drives Sarah crazy, but she can't just ignore it. I understand, but that doesn't make it any easier to live with. Come on, let's shoot."

We worked with our Glock 17s, the department's service pistol, then with the Ithaca shotguns, which were issued to us and lived in the trunks of our unmarked cars. Finally Pete did some work with his Remington 700 that was rigged out as a sniper rifle. He was the closet thing to a sniper the department had. This fifty-yard bay didn't offer too much of a challenge for him. He was putting every round on paper so that a quarter would have touched all of them. After watching for a while, I told him that I needed a restroom break. He nodded and went back to laying shot on top of shot. *His mother-in-law might be a little more circumspect if she saw his bullet groupings*, I thought.

Walking past the large open bay, I saw Matt practicing his running and shooting-from-cover drills. I couldn't see his hits from where I was, but I'd seen him shoot before and had no doubt that every round was on target. Like everything else to do with law enforcement, he seemed to take shooting practice twice as seriously as everyone else.

After taking care of business I came back and stood watching Matt until he took a break. He saw me and lifted his hand in greeting as he walked back to the shooter's bench. After he removed his earmuffs, I filled him in on the meeting with Tim and Margret. He nodded.

He started loading his magazines and looked at me. "I went back over the timeline. There are a few questions there. Checking with the hotel in Tallahassee where Mark was staying, they said he checked in almost five days before he was murdered. Finding out what he did during that time would be helpful." *Damn!* I thought. *Why didn't I think of that?*

"I should have a credit card statement from his bank tomorrow. That'll be a good place to start," I told him.

"I've put most of the information I have on the timeline. I'll email it to you. Fill in what you can. Any information that you can put on it might help us see a pattern. Other than that, I'm stuck waiting for lab reports."

"I'm stuck waiting for suspects. The only people who are still around that are intimately tied to that period, and therefore to each other and the murders, are Dad, Margret and Jim Devries. Margret was in Jacksonville at the time of both her sister's and Mark's murder and Jim was in a coma for both of them. And I don't see an obvious motive for my father."

Matt seemed to be considering my dad. There was no

love lost there. He thought Dad was too lackadaisical about training and preparations for major threats. "We can probably rule out the sheriff," he allowed. "Maybe someone related to those suspects, or maybe we should look into the possibility that they hired someone to do the murders."

"Still need a motive. Several questions come to mind. Why now? What happened to set all of this in motion? That is the biggest and, I think, most important question."

"How does the arson fit into it?"

"I think I might have the answer there. Two possibilities. One, there were pictures and documents stored in the house. Second, as part of a revenge motive."

He nodded and shook his head, picking up his now-loaded magazines. "We'll figure this out, but it's going to take time." He paused and tilted his head toward the bay where we could hear Pete shooting. "Why don't you dump him and get a real partner? You're actually better at this than you appear." He just had to add a bitter taste to what had been a pretty congenial conversation up to this point.

"Pete's a good man." I raised my hand before he could object. "I know how you feel about him, but I'm okay with him."

"Playing cop," he said with a sneer. "Fine. Do what you want." He put his ear protection on and turned back down range.

I walked back to where Pete was looking tired and done in. "About finished?"

"I don't think I have a choice," he said, breathing hard. "I'm out of breath and bullets."

I checked my phone when I got in the car and saw that I'd missed a call from Cara. No message. *Damn.* I called her number.

"Hey."

"I saw you called."

"I had an idea for a date."

"Nice." I saw Pete smirking at me.

"When and where?" I asked.

"Tomorrow? I have Monday afternoon off. Two o'clock."

"Okay. Sure." I'd figure it out somehow. It wasn't like I hadn't worked most of the weekend.

"I'll tell you where when I pick you up. Dress causal."

"I always do. See you then."

"A date?" More leering from Pete. "You're going to be one of us married guys before you know it."

Before I had a chance to give him a smartass answer, I got a text from Dad with a couple other names. Two men and a woman that he could remember being over at the Daniels house. I'd try and track them down when I got home.

Half an hour of Internet investigating and I had numbers for all three names Dad gave me and I actually managed to talk to all three. Sunday evening isn't the worst time to try and get a hold of middle-aged Americans. All of their stories pretty much matched the narrative I already had. Gail Sutherland filled in a few details I hadn't gotten before. She'd been friends with both Dell and Margret though, like everyone else, she'd found it very difficult to be Margret's friend. However, Margret thought enough of Gail that she'd asked her to be her bridesmaid.

"All of us were pretty surprised at how quickly the wedding came about. I remember scrambling to get my dress. Jim just up and proposed to her one day and, within a month, they were married. It didn't surprise any of us when Tim was a month premature. If you know what I mean?"

"You're pretty sure she was pregnant when they got married?"

"Not that big of a deal really. Jim and Margret had been dating off and on for a year. And things could get pretty wild over at the Daniels house when her parents weren't there. Honestly, that's why Jason and I would go over there. Bedrooms are better than backseats. Though plenty of stuff went on in the backseats too. The seventies. Your dad was pretty wild too." She chuckled. You could tell that it was a decade she wouldn't mind reliving. Of course my mind had been damaged by thoughts of my dad doing... whatever.

"You remember Mark Kemper?"

"Sure, he was there for a while. But at some point he just stopped coming by. I think he finally realized that the older kids didn't really want to have him hanging around. He was pretty goofy. Margret played him bad."

"You think he had hurt feelings?"

"Could have. But he was pretty good-natured too. I just remember not seeing him at the house at some point."

"Was he at the wedding?"

"No, it was a small affair. Like I said, put together fast. And I think he'd stopped coming by then."

She didn't have anything else to add. The other two people had even less information.

With Ivy stepping on the keyboard, I did my best to check my email. There was one from Matt. I opened it and looked over the timeline he'd created. He'd started with Mark's arrival at his hotel in Tallahassee four days before he was murdered. Margret was in Jacksonville and seen at various locations on the night that he was killed. It's a good three hours from Jacksonville to Adams County, so she couldn't have done it herself. Did she have someone else do it?

Jim had his stroke two days before the murder, so he was in the hospital at the time. This brought it back to Dad. Location, location, location. He had the opportunity. Certainly had the means. Motive? *No one* seemed to have a motive.

Both Mark Kemper and Dell McDonnell were, by all accounts, two of the nicest people in the world. Did we have a serial killer targeting nice people? If that was the case, then we didn't have to worry because he'd run out of victims soon enough.

Two things kept pointing to the past. There was no

known connection between Mark and Dell except for thirty-five years ago, and a good explanation for why the house was burned down would be the old photos and documents in the area where the fire was started.

I looked back at the timeline. Mark is killed, body is mutilated, the Daniels house is torched, the body is dumped. Dell arrives because of the arson and I question her. She freaks when she finds out about Mark's murder. Back at her hotel she lets someone into her room, and he or she bludgeons Dell to death.

Why was Mark mutilated? My guess was that the killer was an amateur who thought they could disguise the identity of the victim. Maybe they hoped it would be longer before the body was discovered. Or perhaps they just wanted to muddy the waters and hope that a connection wouldn't be made between the murder and the arson.

All of this was making my head spin. It was bedtime. I had to get some work done in the morning so I could come up with a good excuse for playing hooky in the afternoon. Thinking about Cara's phone call made me smile.

CHAPTER EIGHTEEN

I was out of the house before seven, leaving Ivy fed and already taking her morning nap. A front had moved through during the night with a lot of bluster, but little rain. The wind was strong and cold out of the north. I was in a great mood. Of course it had nothing to do with going to work and everything to do with my plans for being a truant that afternoon. I was anxious to see Cara again.

At the office everything was moving at the usual lethargic Monday morning pace. The desk sergeant hardly managed to look up and grunt good morning to me. Everyone I saw was bleary-eyed and grumpy-faced. I'm sure my smiling, perky attitude was appropriately annoying.

After last night's sit-down with the timeline, I'd just about decided to wait for more of the lab results before trying to move forward. There didn't seem to be much choice. Other options included recanvassing all the scenes for witnesses or doing a PSA asking for the public's help. Though we weren't likely to get much out of that.

I was whistling as I checked my emails and then my phone rang. A glance before answering told me it was Cara.

"Hey."

"I'm really sorry about this, but one of the other techs

didn't show up today so I'm going to have to work this afternoon." She genuinely sounded sorry.

"That's okay. I understand." The sound I heard in my head was my spirit being crushed.

"I should be able to get off tomorrow afternoon, if that will work?" That made me feel better. At least she was anxious for us to get together again.

"I'll make it work."

"Cool. Got to go." And she was gone.

Pete came in carrying a bag of fresh pastries. He set the bag on my desk with a cheery "Good morning!"

"Screw you," I replied, grabbing the bag and digging out the biggest, stickiest, fat-filled donut I could find and biting into it.

"Rough night?" he asked, maintaining his good humor.

"Life was grand until five minutes ago."

"When I came in?" He almost sounded hurt.

I waved it away. "Not you."

"The date!"

I scowled and went back to reading my emails and eating my bakery-fresh heart attack.

I tackled the half dozen reports that had been put on my desk. The usual. At first I didn't think a lot about a new arson case. No one had been hurt. The fire hadn't even done too much damage. A storage unit had caught fire and the units on either side suffered damage, but the manager had caught it and called the fire department before it had the chance to get out of hand. But something bugged me about it. I put the auto thefts, a burglary and an assault case aside.

The arson report said that the storage unit belonged to a Dr. Matthew Brook. The name was familiar. I picked up my phone and called his number. A woman answered.

"This is Deputy Macklin. I'm calling about the fire at the doctor's storage unit. Could I speak with him, please?"

"I'm sorry, but the doctor is taking his nap. I'm his caretaker. I might be able to answer your questions."

Nap was not the answer I thought I'd get. "Who am I

speaking with?"

"Pat Clarkson. I've been with the doctor for a number of years."

"How old is the doctor?"

"He'll be eighty-eight in another month," she said. Everything was clearer now.

"Can you tell me what was in the storage unit?"

"Not exactly. Most of the records and materials came from his medical practice. He retired fifteen years ago. I've been to the storage unit once. A couple of years ago he was looking for some documents from when he was in the Army. I can tell you, I'm not surprised there was a fire. The place was a hazard. I saw old X-rays, film, boxes of news clippings, photo albums and a ton of old files."

"Ummm… Is the doctor clear-minded?" I felt bad for asking, but so many older people suffer from Alzheimer's or dementia that you just can't take it for granted that they have a memory left.

"Oh, he's pretty sharp. Has a tendency to get in ruts and repeat the same stories over and over. But other than that, he's fine."

"Terrific. I'm going to check out a couple things and I might want to speak with him."

"Just call ahead and I'm sure we can arrange a time."

We said our goodbyes. I got up and took my coat from the back of my chair. Feeling bad for the way I'd treated Pete, I invited him to ride along with me to U-Keep-It storage.

The place was not very big, just four buildings with units on both sides surrounded by a chain-link fence. The gate was open, but it looked like they locked it at night. Signs wired to the fence gave the hours for access. If you wanted after-hours access there was a number you could call. A nice doublewide had a sign reading "office" on it, but it clearly functioned as someone's residence too. I parked next to it and Pete and I went in.

A nice-looking middle-aged woman sat at a desk. "Can I

help you, gentlemen?" she asked with the air of professionalism that you might expect at a New York law firm.

"We're with the sheriff's office. We're investigating the fire you had last night."

"I'm glad you're here. My father owns the place. He's sleeping right now, having been up all night." *Does everyone but me get to take naps?* I wondered.

"I can show you the unit. It's a real mess between the fire and the water hoses." She came around the desk carrying a set of keys. "The water did a lot more damage. We had to cut the owner's lock off, of course, and put on one of our own. Have you talked to Dr. Brook?" She never stopped talking from the time we entered the office until we stood in front of the wet, blackened mess that used to be the doctor's memories and records.

"We saw CCTV cameras in the front. Are there any back here?" I asked, looking around.

"No, only on the front gate and the office, which is also my dad's home."

Pete looked around the fence while I tried to find something readable inside the storage unit. "Here!" he yelled.

I went over to the chain-link fence where he was holding part of it off the ground. Someone had carefully cut the wire so they could crawl in. Pete pointed to a few pieces of thread on the jagged end of the cuts.

"Looks like he left some evidence this time."

I used my phone to call for the crime scene techs. Shantel called me back and I told her the situation and what I wanted them to collect. They were out the door before we hung up.

Everything in the unit was toast. What wasn't burned had turned into a soggy mush. Was it connected to the other arson and the murders? Seemed like a longshot, though it was hard to imagine why someone would torch an old doctor's storage unit. Unless they got the wrong unit. In the dark, under stress, that would be easy enough to do. And it was very believable that an ex-husband or lover might torch their significant other's stuff. That would fall under business as usual.

I'd talk to the doctor first chance I got to try and rule out, or in, a connection with the murders, but right now I had other cases that needed attention while the murder investigations simmered. I spent the afternoon dealing with my inbox.

Dad called at four to let me know that Jim Devries had passed away and that the funeral was scheduled for Thursday. I told him I'd go to the funeral with him.

I was on call Monday night and had to work a couple incidents—one a domestic where the wife was put in the hospital and another call about a car-jacking that turned into a drug thing by the time I got there. I took my time coming in Tuesday morning with the idea that I'd check email and finish the reports from the night before, then make an excuse for heading out for my date with Cara.

I decided to call Dr. Brook to see if he had time for me to visit and maybe I could clear up the questions about the fire at his storage unit. Talking to the doctor would let me skip out with a clear conscience.

When the nurse picked up the phone I knew something was wrong.

"This is Deputy Macklin. I called yesterday," I said, hearing sniffles on the other end of the line.

"I… he… I'm afraid the doctor passed away last night," she said and my heart dropped.

"Has the body been moved?"

"What? Yes. Marshall's came and… picked him up about an hour ago." She was referring to Marshall's Funeral Home.

"Don't touch anything in the room. I'm coming straight over," I ordered. Confused, she agreed. I texted Matt to meet me there. I couldn't see how this could be a coincidence, arson and death going hand in hand again. I called Marshall's Funeral Home, identified myself and told them not to do anything with the body.

As I drove I looked at my phone sitting on the dash. Should I call Cara or not? I couldn't see any option. When viewed with the knowledge that there had been another murder/arson combo just a week earlier, it seemed probable that the doctor's death was related. Even if it wasn't, it would take me a few hours to convince myself of that. Cara took it pretty well and we agreed to postpone our date again, agreeing we'd try to reschedule for Saturday.

Matt was waiting for me in front of the doctor's house. The house was in one of the best and oldest neighborhoods in Calhoun, standing back from the street on an acre lot. The two-story Victorian had the look of a home well-maintained for years, but becoming a bit neglected now.

There was already a black wreath on the door courtesy of Marshall's. Before I knocked, I gave Matt all the details, and he agreed that the death needed a thorough investigation. A large sturdy woman in a dark dress answered the door.

"I'm Pat," she said.

"Deputies Macklin and Greene," I said. She ushered us in. We followed her to the second door on the right.

"We had to move him down here when it became too difficult for him to climb the stairs." The room had obviously once been a library. Recent additions to the library included an old, well-made wooden double bed, a bedside table and a chest of drawers. The bed's covers were pulled back and soiled, which created an unpleasant smell in the room.

"I'm sorry for the... mess. You told me to leave everything the way it was."

"You did the right thing." The windows were open. "Did you open the windows?"

"Yes, I'm sorry, I did that while I was waiting for the funeral home."

"Were they unlocked?" Matt beat me to the question.

"Yes. This time of year the doctor would have them open

155

a lot. He always swore by fresh air. Told everyone to get out more and to keep their houses as open as possible. He followed his own advice."

We went over to the windows and what I saw chilled me. A muddy mark on the carpet. It was so near the window and so far away from the bed that it was hard to imagine it being made by anyone entering the room from the main part of the house. The mud appeared to be fresh.

Matt got on the phone to the coroner and then called Marshall's. I phoned Shantel and told her we had more work for her.

"I'm going to start expecting a separate check from you personally," she grumbled good-naturedly.

At four o'clock we wrapped up the evidence collection at the house. At six I got a call from Dr. Darzi saying that a very preliminary examination of the body suggested smothering, most likely with a pillow. All the bed linens, including the pillowcases, had been bagged and tagged. I emailed the lab to pay special attention to the cases. I also called Shantel and asked her to send someone over to the house to pick up the pillows.

CHAPTER NINETEEN

Wednesday was spent writing the report and going over the evidence in the doctor's case. This included tracking down CCTV footage from banks, public buildings, fast food restaurants and anywhere else we could think of that might cover some of the approaches to the storage unit or the doctor's house. We hoped that by comparing them with footage from the cameras that were within a couple of blocks of the warehouse where Mark Kemper was killed and the motel where Dell was bludgeoned, we might find a vehicle or pedestrian common to all three or at least two of the scenes. A lot of time spent looking in a haystack that might or might not have a needle in it.

Pete helped me dig up a couple nurses who had worked with the doctor when he had his practice. Dr. Brook ran a general practice from his office in Calhoun from 1960 until 2000. The Devries family had been patients of his, as had the Danielses. Dad admitted that he'd gone to him a few times before he married Mom, before she decided she wanted a younger doctor when she was pregnant. So there appeared to be at least some connection between the doctor and the Daniels group. But in a small town, was that surprising?

Thursday morning, I dressed for the funeral. Accompanying my dad and paying respects to a man I'd known my whole life were my primary reasons for attending. However, it also afforded me the opportunity to observe Margret Devries. At least I assumed she'd be there. I couldn't believe that egotistical blowhard would miss the dramatic opportunities offered by a funeral.

Dad wanted me to pick him up at his house. I waited in the car, hoping he'd come out so I could avoid Mauser slobbering all over my best suit. No luck. After ten minutes he still hadn't come outside. I got out of the car and had reached the midway point between the car and the house when the door opened and Mauser came charging across the lawn.

"Do your business," Dad shouted from the door.

Mauser headed straight for me. The car was too far away. I bent at the knees and prepared to be hit. The huge animal lifted his front feet and smashed into me. I kept upright, but he managed to smear the front of my dark suit with muddy paws. The greeting over, he slammed his head into me in one last show of recognition and affection, then headed off into the bushes to attend to his business.

Dad came out of the house looking well groomed and somber. "Mauser, good boy, come here."

Mauser didn't even look back. He was on the trail of a squirrel, armadillo or some other animal that he would never catch. His babysitter came out and told Dad to go on and that he'd get Mauser back into the house. With leash in hand, the young man started following the dog through the bushes. Dad got in the car with a grunt of greeting for me.

The funeral was at the largest church in town, Calhoun First Baptist. Jim and his son were Methodist, but the church they attended wouldn't be able to hold the crowd of people wanting to pay their respects. In one way the family had been fortunate in the way that Jim had died. The time on life support had given them the opportunity to prepare for the mammoth service that a cornerstone of the community deserved. Thousands of people in the county owed Jim a debt of thanks for jobs and support that they would have been hard put to find anywhere else. The parking lot was full.

Tim greeted us at the door. "Thank you for coming, Sheriff Macklin," he said in a mournful tone. It was obviously not an act. Tim and his father had been dedicated to each other. The only time Tim had spent away from the farm was the four years he attended school in Gainesville. As soon as he received his degree in agricultural business he was back in Adams County, working with his dad.

We went into the church and took our seats midway between the altar and the doors. Sure enough, I could see Margret sitting in the second pew from the front. I guess even she knew that it would be inappropriate for her, as the ex-wife, to sit in the front pew. Tilly sat next to her. The two heads would come together for a few minutes and then part, until one or the other thought of some other interesting tidbit to gossip about.

I watched them throughout the service and an idea grew. Margret was our best suspect simply by association. In one way or another, she knew every one of the victims. It wasn't much to go on, but I had a hunch she was up to something. The reason we hadn't looked at Margret seriously as a suspect, besides the fact we didn't have a motive, was that she had iron-tight alibis for both Kemper and Dell. But she had an ally who *did* have the opportunity.

When the family broke up, Tilly went with her mom. Would Tilly kill for her mother? She certainly had the same type of take-no-prisoners personality. But that was a long way from being an instrument of murder. What would we get if we brought Tilly in for questioning? Sitting there in the pew, I decided to find out.

As soon as I was in the car with Dad, heading for the gravesite, I pulled out my phone and called Matt. I told him what I was thinking and asked him to check Tilly out. Dad overheard my conversation and frowned at me.

"You can't bring her in for a couple of days. Her father just died."

"One, she didn't look like she was taking it that hard—"

"That's not the point," Dad interrupted in an agitated voice.

I raised my hand to calm him. "I know I have to tread lightly here. But point two is that now is the perfect time if she is emotionally off-base."

"How do you think Tim is going to take it?" Dad wasn't going to let this go.

"I would think that he'd want to find the person who murdered his aunt." I raised my hand again to stop him. "What we can do is ask her to come in and talk with us. If she says no, we'll give it a couple days and then bring a little force to bear." I looked over at him.

He didn't look happy. "I know you're trying to do your job. But Jim was one of my best friends. Harassing one of his children is not something I want my office to be responsible for. Do you understand me? I'm talking now as your boss, not as your father. As your father, I'm asking you to move very cautiously. I saw that girl two days after she was born. I've been to more of her birthday parties than yours."

That last was the truth and it kinda stung. It also got the point across that Dad would not want her to be hurt.

The procession had reached the cemetery. I followed another car onto the side of an internal road and cut the engine. Turning to Dad, I asked, "And if I find evidence that she had some involvement in the murders?"

"You don't have to ask that. You know damn well that I won't let my friendship with Jim or his daughter stop me from doing my duty, or make me stop you from doing yours. All I ask is that, until it is clear she is in some way responsible, you be gentle. That's all I'm saying." He opened the door and got out.

It was a warm, dry November day standing beside the graveside. A small awning from Marshall's covered the casket and the hole that was already dug, but discreetly covered with Astroturf. The graveside service was mercifully short. Even so, I was sweating under the sun in my dark suit.

Dropping a still disgruntled Dad off at his house, I changed and went back to the office. Matt was at his desk and I pulled him aside.

"Find out anything about Tilly Devries?"

"She's got a few charges on her record. Two for drunk driving. The worst is an aggravated assault conviction from an incident where she attacked a bouncer at a Jacksonville Beach night club. She pleaded guilty and received a suspended sentence. The club refused to drop the charges because they claimed she had attacked employees before. I say we bring her in and talk to her."

"I do too. But her father was buried today. We need to tread softly." I repeated Dad's words.

Matt nodded, but didn't look satisfied. "She'll be more off balance now. It's the perfect time to question her," he said, echoing me.

"I hear you. I thought we could go out there tomorrow morning and talk to her."

"We really need to try and get her in here where we have the home field advantage."

"How about we ask her to come in? I'll call her and tell her we want to go over a few things concerning her Aunt Dell."

"If she refuses?"

"I guess that would tell us something. If she does, then we go out there and put some pressure on her and see how she reacts."

"It's always a give and take anyway. Sure, we can do it that way." Matt seemed accepting.

Having a suspect, or at least a person of interest, was a relief. If, and it was a big if, Margret and Tilly were involved in the murders of Mark Kemper, Dell McDonnell and Dr. Brook, covering up something in the past seemed like the only reasonable explanation.

I considered the Kemper murder. What could he have known? Did he come to town to blackmail Margret? That could have been why he was upset or nervous. But his finances had checked out. He didn't have any unusual debt. We had checked the hospitals he sold to and none of them had reported any drugs missing or other irregularities that might have suggested that Mark had a problem that could have gotten him in trouble and in need of cash. No one who knew him said anything but good things about him.

There was a similar problem with Dell. She was too good and had too few issues. Of course, with a family member anything was possible. But Margret and Dell had played the same roles all their lives—Margret was the hardass and Dell was the sweetheart. Why would Margret fear or hate Dell enough to have Tilly kill her?

I decided to stop thinking about it because, the more I did, the less I liked the idea of Margret being the puppet master manipulating Tilly. Hopefully talking to Tilly in the morning would either disprove the idea or give us a launching point for a more thorough look into the theory.

The next morning Matt was waiting for me at my desk. I called Tilly's cell phone and got no answer, so Matt wandered off while I kept trying. When I didn't get her around nine, I decided to call Tim and find out where Tilly was.

"She's probably still asleep," he said, sounding short of breath. "I'm loading hay to take to the feed store. If it's important, I could go up to the house."

"When do you think she'll be up?"

"She and her mother usually don't get up much before noon. They went into Tallahassee last night and didn't get back until late." There was an edge to his voice. And referring to Margret as "her mother" was a slight he'd emphasized.

Finding out that she went into Tallahassee partying the day of her father's funeral took a lot of my sympathy and dumped it in the trash. "Don't worry about it. I'll just keep calling."

"What did you want to talk with her about?" he asked.

Here is where I needed to be careful. I didn't want Tim to think we were jumping to conclusions.

"I just want to go over a few things. Mostly about her relationship with her aunt and to make sure she hadn't known Mark."

"How could she have known Mark?"

"I don't know. That's why I need to ask her some questions. It's always possible that she met him at a bar or through his or her work."

"I don't think she hangs out at hospitals, and she doesn't have a real job of her own. So I don't think she could have met him," he insisted.

"You're probably right. They're just questions that we need to ask in order to do our due diligence," I said, making us sound like the bureaucrats that we often are.

"Yeah, okay, I can understand that. Just keep calling back. When she wakes up, the first thing she'll look for is her phone."

Tilly finally picked up my call an hour later.

"Who is this?" she answered. Her mother's child.

"Tilly, this is Larry Macklin. I hate to bother you, but we need to ask a few more questions. Could you come down to the sheriff's office?"

"When? Today?" She made it sound like I'd asked her to walk through fire.

"Yes, I was hoping you could make it in today." I was doing my best to sound open and inviting. "It won't take long and then we won't have to bother you anymore." I offered her the hope of never having to hear my voice again.

"I'm pretty busy…" She was playing hard to get.

"We just need some information so that we can move forward with the investigation. I know how much you want us to find the person who killed your aunt." An appeal to the heart if she had one.

"When?"

"At your convenience."

"It's not really convenient, but I can be there about one?" she said, very tentatively.

"That would be perfect. I'll look forward to seeing you." I put as much butter on the bread as possible. I didn't want her to think for a minute that we viewed her as anything but a victim in all of this.

I told Matt that I had a bite and that we'd see if we could reel it in.

One o'clock turned to one-fifteen and then one-thirty. At one-forty I got a call from the front desk that I had a visitor. I picked Matt up from his desk on my way to the front.

Tilly was wearing a shirt and a pair of shorts that suggested she was looking for attention. Her face, on the other hand, just looked annoyed. We ushered her into the conference room.

"How well did you know your Aunt Dell?" I had decided to start off with the easy questions and move on to the tougher ones.

"Pretty well. I saw her sometimes when I was growing up. Dad even liked her. He was always glad to have her and her husband come down for the holidays. And, of course, she came down and took care of Grans and Grams. Grams is living with her... Well, I guess with Uncle Mike now." This seemed to make a dent in her stunted emotional maturity.

"After I moved to Jacksonville with Mom, Aunt Dell came and stayed with us a few times a year. Mom didn't get along with her too well, but I liked her. She always told me how pretty I was and that I could go into modeling or something. Not like Mom. She's always harping on my weight. Do I look fat? Mom's one to talk. Jesus, she's got these huge varicose veins in the—"

"If we could stay on course here." If I hadn't interrupted her, we would have been off on wild tangents all day. "Your mom didn't get along with your aunt? Was there anything in particular that they argued about?"

"They never argued."

"But you said they didn't get along?"

"No, I said that Mom didn't get along with Aunt Dell. You should listen better. Of course Mom doesn't really get along with anyone. You might have noticed. She's in this big fight right now with her neighbor in Jacksonville. The woman, her name is Betty, she's building this boat dock and—"

"Okay, so there wasn't anything in particular that your mother had a problem with?"

"With Aunt Dell? No, just the usual, always telling her she dressed like a slob and that she should lose weight. But, like I said, that's Mom. Of course everything she said was true. Aunt Dell's clothes were crap. Like she bought them from Walmart or something."

"Why'd you go to live with your mom? How old were you, twelve?" I asked.

"Are you kidding? Dad never did anything but work on that stupid farm and go to church. And Tim is… was his mini-me, for sure."

"Think hard, did you ever meet Mark Kemper?" Matt put a photo of Kemper down on the table in front of her. "This is a pretty recent picture. Maybe you met him when you were younger?"

I'll give her credit. She looked hard at the photo and took her time answering. "I don't care much for gay guys. He even looks gay in this picture. I never saw him before. Like I said, I don't pay much attention to gay guys, but I think I'd remember him. I can't believe Mom dated him. Damn."

Matt stepped up. "It would be helpful to know where you were Monday night, November second."

Tilly sat up, her body tensing. I guess we'd moved into "good cop, bad cop" mode.

"Are you serious?" Tilly ended the sentence by dropping her jaw and staring at Matt.

"We have to cross the t's and dot the i's. If you can tell us where you were, and it checks out, then that's one less person we have to keep an eye on."

"What? Like you're watching me?" Her mouth was still hanging open.

"We have two murders. We keep an eye on everyone associated with any murder until we can be sure they have no connection with them. Understand?" Matt spoke fast and with an attitude. He was ramping this up way more than I thought was necessary.

"This is bullshit. Why would I even kill him? Do I look like someone who could shoot a man with a shotgun?"

I had to step in here, because I'd thought about this. "I know that your dad took you dove and quail hunting as soon as you were old enough to hold a shotgun."

"That was a long time ago."

Leon had said he saw a *man* point the gun at Mark Kemper, but the mind can fill in details and the brain will try to make sense of things even if that means changing reality to make it fit. If our witness couldn't imagine a woman with a shotgun, then when he saw one in the dark and from a distance, his mind might have just changed the facts to fit what his brain told him he should be seeing. That's one of the many reasons that eyewitness testimony is notoriously unreliable.

"Money is always a good motive," Matt continued. "You don't work. Did your mom offer you money to kill him?"

"I don't need money. My dad left me half of his. And you might remember, I already knew that Dad probably wouldn't survive." She at least had the good grace to say that last a little sadly. I was very surprised to hear that Jim had left half

166

his estate to Tilly. I'd imagined that all, or at least most, of it would go to Tim and I said as much.

"Shows what you know. Dad didn't leave a will. It was one more thing he was weird about. So half goes to me and half to Tim."

"Just tell us where you were on the night of November second and we can move on." Matt leaned on the table and got in her face.

"I don't know, partying, I guess."

"On a Monday night?"

"Maybe at home. I don't have to answer your stupid questions."

"That's true. You can walk out of here and we'll put you at the top of our list."

Her mouth opened wide again. "No way. What the hell? You can't do that."

"Just answer the question."

"I don't know. Let me think. Monday, what, a couple of weeks ago?" She pulled out her phone and looked at her messages. "Let me see."

Matt loomed over her.

"I was at a bar!" she said triumphantly. "The Den, in Tallahassee." She showed her phone to him. I gently took it from her. There were a number of texts with selfies of her at a bar between the hours of eleven and two in the morning.

"Who are these people with you?" I asked, and she rattled off the names of half a dozen people. Young, dumb and drunk from the looks of the photos. "Hold on. Write them down with phone numbers." I slid my pad over to her and gave her back her phone. She wrote down names and numbers after looking them up on her phone.

I glanced over the list. "Thanks. Does your mother have anyone else that she relies on? A best friend? Is she dating anyone?"

"She broke up with some old guy a couple of months ago. He was rich. If they don't have money, they don't count, is the way she dates. She told me once she didn't want arm candy, she wanted a deep wallet." Her voice trailed off.

"Okay, we appreciate you coming in."

"What a bunch of crap," she threw back at us on her way out.

"That was a fucking waste of time," Matt said after she left.

"You didn't have to pull out the thumbscrews," I told him.

"Give me a break. If she'd been guilty, I would have gotten a confession out of her."

"You can get a confession out of most people if you browbeat them long enough. Look at the Norfolk Four." The Norfolk Four were four sailors who confessed to a 1997 rape and murder. It became clear after several years and the confession of another man, who was a known rapist, that the confessions were false. Through little more than sleep deprivation and constant aggressive questioning, the four young men had been willing to confess to a heinous crime they hadn't committed.

Matt gave me a withering look and walked out. Back to square one. I considered all of the information. If we had been talking about the murder of Jim Devries, then she'd just given me a great motive for her or Tim. Maybe I'd check with Jim's doctors and make darn sure that there wasn't any chance his death could have been anything but natural causes. A call to Jim's lawyer was in order too. A man of his wealth not having a will seemed crazy, even knowing how much he hated contracts.

CHAPTER TWENTY

I followed up with two of Jim's doctors and left a message for his lawyer. The doctors assured me that the hemorrhagic stroke Jim suffered was a natural event. Of course they couldn't just tell me that. They had to explain that a hemorrhagic stroke differed from an ischemic stroke. The hemorrhagic stroke is caused when a blood vessel in the brain ruptures. The ischemic occurs when a blood clot lodges in a vessel in the brain and blocks the flow of blood. Hemorrhagic are less common and generally cause more damage.

So much for making his death out to be a murder, even though I had already begun to map out the events. Jim is somehow given a stroke; Mark knew something and was killed; same goes for Dell; and then Dr. Brook was killed because he had some knowledge of the medical condition that was exploited to cause the death. What was really upsetting was that, as crazy as that scenario sounded, it was better than anything else I'd come up with. But it was all for naught if Jim's death was natural.

The doctors did give me one small opening, saying stress was possibly a contributing factor. However, there was no way that someone could have known Jim was susceptible to a stroke, and certainly it wasn't credible that you could count on him having a massive stroke just because he was put in a stressful situation.

My phone rang.

"What the hell are you doing accusing my sister of killing Mark Kemper?"

"Tim, we had to look at all the possibilities. She's cleared now."

"You demanded an alibi!" No room for doubt about how upset he was.

"That's not exactly the way it was. I admit that Deputy Greene might have leaned on her a little heavy, but we're fighting an uphill battle with these murders. I will say that you need to consider the fact that these deaths and arsons are very close to your family."

"Do you think I need to be reminded that my aunt was murdered?"

"No, I just meant that there could be some danger to your immediate family. Since we don't have any idea who's committing these murders, or why."

"Is that some kind of threat? If we don't cooperate, we could be next?"

This wasn't going well. He didn't seem to want to be calmed down. *Maybe this is his way of venting all of the emotions that must have been building up with the death of his father, the murder of his aunt and the arrival of his mother. He probably needs to be careful that* he *doesn't have a stroke.* Not a very kind thought. I decided to take another tack.

"You have every right to be mad. I should have told you why we asked your sister to come in. But we thought it would be better to just do it and get the ugly job done as fast as possible. Is your sister still upset?"

"What do you think?" He was finally cooling down. "I know my sister has her flaws, but killing people isn't one of them." Hearing him say it *did* make our suspecting her sound stupid.

"We had to take her off the list of suspects. And we have.

Her alibi checked out."

"I guess we should be grateful for that." He just sounded irritated now, not like he might go ballistic at any moment. "Am I on your list too?"

"In an investigation like this, we look at everyone." I wanted to ask where he was on that Monday night, but I didn't think now was the time. Besides, like everyone else, what motive did he have?

"I guess you'll just have to keep me on your list. With Dad in the hospital I was going back and forth between the hospital and the house the day Kemper was killed."

"I understand." *Best let it drop for now.* We said our goodbyes and hung up.

What a day. But tomorrow was my date with Cara and this time I wasn't going to let anything stop me from going out with her. Dead bodies be damned. They could just pile up if no one else wanted to deal with them. I called dispatch and told them that if anything came up tomorrow, the word was that I was unreachable. Lunch for everyone on Monday if I wasn't disturbed.

I decided to stop by Dad's on the way home. It was a preemptive measure: just in case Tim called him, I wanted to let Dad know what went down. Dad's car was in the driveway so I let myself in, shouting to the house that I was there. The expected brutal greeting from Mauser didn't happen. This was explained when I went into the living room and found him chewing contentedly on a huge frozen bone. Like any veteran law enforcement officer, when he was eating, he was off duty. He barely lifted his eyes when I came into the room and sat down on the sofa.

Dad walked in, fresh from a shower and dressed casually, which meant that he was wearing old-man shorts with a polo shirt, everything in hideous colors because he always bought the ones on the clearance racks.

I told him how the interview with Tilly went. He sat there

frowning. I couldn't tell if he was grinding his teeth or if it was just Mauser tearing his bone apart.

"I told you so."

"Thanks, Dad, I appreciate you not saying 'I told you so.'"

"If it's necessary in the line of duty, I expect you to do whatever you have to to bring about law and order and to come home alive. But if you can avoid it, I would appreciate you not pissing off the richest and most influential people in the county less than a year out from an election."

"Yeah, yeah. I know." I hated the politics of the job. I know Dad did too, but that was the reality. I'd never seen him do anything wrong in order to keep his job, but I'd seen him do things he didn't want to do.

I stayed and had dinner with him—leftover spaghetti and garlic bread. Ivy was put out with me for coming home after eight, but I tried to placate her with the idea of turkey for a week after Thanksgiving.

Cara called to make sure that we were still on for tomorrow. I assured her that nothing was going to stop me from being with her.

"Where are we going?"

"On Monday I was planning on surprising you, but now after a couple of false starts I'm just going to tell you. I thought we'd go to Wakulla Springs."

The springs were an hour away, about twenty miles south of Tallahassee.

"I haven't been there in years. I loved it as a kid," I said sincerely.

"I haven't ever been."

"I wish I'd thought of it." Picking a state park rather than a posh restaurant raised her up a dozen pegs on my score board. I was beginning to worry that I might not live up to her standards. We agreed that I'd pick her up at ten.

I really wanted to make a great second impression. The weather was neither warm nor cold, so I didn't have to make any major clothing decisions. I checked the car and cleared out the trash and some of the paperwork. I'd gas it up before I picked her up in the morning. I checked Google maps to be sure I knew where I was going. Ivy followed me around the whole time.

"Guys worry about stuff too. We aren't all Neanderthals, or at least we aren't all *always* Neanderthals," I told her. She chose that moment to sit on her back, bend forward and start cleaning her butt. I knew this was not a coincidence. "Yeah, maybe you won't be getting quite as much turkey next week." But she knew it was an idle threat.

I got a text from Eddie Saturday morning as I was making last-minute preparations to pick up Cara. It was simple enough: *Found guy who was asked by guy about arson.* I just wasn't in the mood for a texting exchange with my CI, especially when it started out that vague. It could wait until the evening.

Cara looked beautiful, wearing a sundress in a mix of bold colors. It was a bright day and her red hair glowed in the sunlight. As we drove I wished I had a convertible. Cara would have looked perfect smiling up at the blue sky with her hair flying behind her.

Wakulla Springs in the fall, even on the weekend, is off the beaten path. There were a few cars in the parking lot, but it wasn't crowded. We walked through the old lodge, admiring the curiosities of days gone by and imagining ourselves in a world where Florida was still exotic.

"I sometimes feel that I was born in the wrong time," Cara said dreamily. "I guess that's pretty common."

"I think it speaks to our desire for the romance of a time and place when the world still seemed filled with mysteries you might reach out and touch."

"These days all the things to be discovered seem to require powerful telescopes or deep-water submersibles."

According to the plaque on the wall the lodge had been built in 1937.

"Hard to imagine Hitler had taken control of Germany by then and the world waited to learn what fate had in mind," I said.

"Aren't you the romantic?" She put her arm through mine.

"I wanted to study history. It fascinates me. Reading about people in the past and imagining what it would be like to stand in their shoes and face the daunting tasks without knowing if you would be successful or not..."

"Don't *we* face huge challenges which leave us unsure of the future?" she asked as we walked outside and strolled through the grounds, the maze of live oak branches overhead mottling the sunlight.

"Somehow our times seem less dramatic. I don't know... Maybe it's that the number of people and the complexities make everything less clear. A hundred years ago, if a man or woman wanted to go somewhere and reinvent themselves, they could. It was possible to leave your old reality behind and pioneer a new life. Good luck today leaving your past and starting over."

"I know what you mean. My parents lived a freer life in their hippy world than I think is possible today. Even they've settled down. Is there something you'd like to escape?"

"No... I'm not exactly trapped."

"But not free? You told me how you became a deputy. It's not too late to do something else. Go back to school, study history. Do whatever you want."

I looked at her and, for a moment, she made me believe that the world *did* hold endless possibilities. Maybe if you are with the right person they can help you to move toward the life you want. Or maybe if you're with the right person, the life you have is the life you want.

"Or I can just keep doing what I'm doing until I'm too old to remember that I wanted to do something else," I said with a chuckle.

"Love the one you're with if you can't be with the one you love," she said.

"I like the 'love the one you're with' part," I said, turning to her. I leaned in and she raised up on her toes so that our lips met. The kiss was perfect. We parted and looked into each other's eyes.

"Let's take the boat tour," I said quickly. I didn't want to say anything that would spoil the kiss, and if the silence hadn't been filled with some banality I would have been telling her my feelings when it was too early to know what my feelings really were.

"Great," she said, giving no indication how the kiss had affected her beyond the sparkle in her eyes. She let go of my hand and started running down the bank toward the boat docks. I didn't catch up with her until we reached the little office that sold tickets. We had to wait for a while until the next boat went out. We passed the time looking at the movie posters on the wall. Starting in the 1940s, the springs had been used by Hollywood to film underwater scenes for various movies. There were posters for Tarzan movies and *Airport '77*.

"You aren't going to believe this, but that is one of my favorite films," I said, pointing to a poster for *The Creature from the Black Lagoon*. "It was Dad's favorite growing up. He had it on VHS when I was a kid and a couple times a year he'd ask me if I wanted to have dinner in the Black Lagoon. He'd bring home a pizza and turn off all the lights. For dessert we'd make wild and crazy sundaes. Those were some of the best times I had with my dad.

"Not long after I started working for the department, I had one of those really bad days when I saw some stuff that nobody should have to see. I asked Dad how he decompressed after one of those days. He told me he'd put *The Creature* on and eat pizza and ice cream with his son."

Cara put her arm around me. A park ranger came in and told us the tour was ready to leave.

A dozen people were on board as the boat glided over the crystal clear waters of the springs. As we turned and headed down river, the guide pointed out the birds and wildlife along the banks.

"This is amazing. I love Florida springs," Cara said, looking at the sunbathing alligators and the anhingas drying their wings. "My parents used to take me tubing down the Ichetucknee River a couple times a year."

"Your parents sound very interesting."

"If you find hippies interesting." She laughed. "Actually, they're more serious than that makes them sound. They do a lot of good work. I had to work hard and spent a lot of time helping others when I was growing up. They gave me a great start in life. But that's not to say we didn't have issues. Dad can be a bit autocratic. He knows what is right and has little patience for those that take a little longer to see the light. Mom, well, she has a tendency to go off on her own tangents. Sometimes at inconvenient moments. Wherever we lived, we were surrounded with her projects. She finished a lot of them and, when she did, they were amazing. But a lot more never went much beyond an initial manic phase." She stopped and looked at me. "I hope I'm not making them sound too odd."

"No. You're making them sound unique. Like the kind of people that could raise an amazing woman." I kissed her lightly on the lips. We spent another twenty minutes listening to the tour and spotting the alligators.

Walking back toward the lodge, I asked Cara if she wanted to get lunch in the dining room.

"I'm famished," she said and started pulling my arm like an excited kid. I was having the best day in years. I tried to tell myself that I was just feeling the first rush of infatuation, but it felt like more than that. I wasn't someone to get lost in emotion easily, which added to the feeling that this was something very special. I was soon to be reminded that an amazing day can explode in an instant.

We were finishing lunch when Cara saw a small flyer advertising wedding planning services at the lodge.

"This would be a beautiful place for a wedding," she blurted out. That sentence spooked me. *Where is this going?* my mind wondered as I signaled our waiter for the check.

She went on, "I've got some friends that just got engaged. This would be perfect." *Oh, okay.* "One of them works at the vet. He is really funny. Whenever I'm feeling like crap because an animal has taken a turn for the worse or a client has been a real asshole, he knows how to cheer me up. His fiancée is quite a bit older than he is, and when he was first telling me about the guy I wasn't too sure. But Rick is just as nice as Terry." She looked at me. "I'm prattling, aren't I?"

"No. I'm interested in your friends. Actually, I'm interested in learning everything about you." I tried to make it sound light-hearted, but I was serious.

"He was talking about finding a place yesterday. It would be neat to come here for their wedding."

"Maybe we could stay here. They have rooms." *Oh, no, you moron, you went too far!* my inner voice screamed.

"That might be nice." And she gave me a smile. "I'll have to suggest the lodge to Terry. He and Rick are planning everything with the help of Rick's son. He's like fifteen and is so excited for his dad."

"What did you say?" Something she said caused a weird flash in my mind.

"What? I said I'd tell Terry about the lodge." She looked puzzled by my reaction.

"No, not that. Something else… You said that Rick had a boy, a child?"

"Yes. So?"

"He's gay."

"Right, so…?"

"He's gay and has a child." A bright light went off in my brain and in an instant I realized that Margret Devries was in grave danger. I jumped out of my seat. "I'll be right back."

I stepped outside, trying to find Margret's number as fast as I could. Adrenaline was pulsing through me as I dialed, muttering the mantra *answer, answer, answer.* Nothing. I texted her: *Stay away from your son. Go immediately to the sheriff's office. I'll meet you there.*

I started to put my phone back in my pocket when it rang. It was Margret.

"Turn on FaceTime," came Tim's voice, dark and low.

"What?"

"You have an iPhone. Turn on FaceTime. Don't do anything else. Just find the icon and turn it on or my mother dies."

I had used FaceTime exactly twice when I first got the phone. But I figured it out. I could see Tim and behind him, taped to a chair, was his mother. I couldn't tell where they were.

"Where are you?" Tim asked as though he was echoing my thoughts.

"Wakulla Springs."

This seemed to take him a minute to process. "Okay, here's what I want you to do. Keep the phone on FaceTime. Keep the camera on your face at all times. If you hang up, she dies. If you lose your signal, she dies. If you try in any way to alert someone, she dies. You are going to come to me."

"I can't guarantee that I won't lose my signal. I'm down in Wakulla County."

"I'd suggest you stick to the main roads." He was hard and cold. I'd never seen or heard him like this.

"I have a date. She's in the restaurant. I have to let her know I'm leaving." I turned the phone so he could see her through the dining room's large French windows. "If I don't, she may call my father or someone else."

"Get her attention, wave, smile and leave. Don't go back in the restaurant."

"But…"

"Or she dies."

I had a totally selfish moment when I thought, *Let the horrible woman die. I'm going back and finishing my date.* But that wasn't possible. It was easy to get Cara's attention as she'd been watching me while I talked on the phone.

"Keep the phone on your face. Wave and smile and then walk around the building to the parking lot."

I waved and Cara smiled and waved back. It broke my heart. I walked away as fast as I could.

"You don't have to do this. I know…"

"Shut up." He cut me off. "I'm not going to talk about it. Just get in your car and drive. Keep your phone on your face."

"Listen, that's going to be very difficult."

"Do I give a damn? Figure it out."

CHAPTER TWENTY-ONE

It took me a minute to get the phone set up on the dash mount so that it kept my face in frame while I drove. My mind was working, trying to figure out the most populated route home with the hopes that I could keep the signal. I looked at the battery icon and saw that the charge was 94%... Should be more than enough for the hour-plus drive home.

"Where am I going?"

"I'll direct you once you're back in Adams County."

My muscles were aching from gripping the steering wheel when I finally crossed into Adams County. I'd tried to come up with a way out of this, but everything ended with Margret Devries dead. And probably with Tim dead too. I'd tried getting him to talk to me several times, but each time he just cut me off. His voice was flat and emotionless. I tried to ignore my phone as it rang off and on.

Tim finally started giving me directions, heading me toward Calhoun. After a few more miles and several more turns, I realized I was coming in on the south side heading for the area around the warehouse where Mark Kemper had been shot. When I was close, Tim gave me two more turns that led me to a spot several blocks over from the warehouse and railroad tracks, but still within the industrial area.

"Get out of your car and come into the building you see to your right," he told me. It was an old tobacco warehouse. "Use the office door."

The rusty door with its faded sign reading "office" was at the top of five concrete steps. I opened it and stepped into a moldy, dusty room filled with old metal desks and ratty leather chairs. It was obvious that the place hadn't been used for years.

"Take your gun out of your holster and place it in the desk. Show it to me on the phone and then close the drawer."

"I was on a date. I don't have a gun." I pulled my shirt out of my pants and showed him that I wasn't wearing a gun inside my waistband.

"Bullshit. Let me see your ankles." Busted. I took the PPK/S off of my ankle, showing him as I put it in a drawer. After he'd made sure that I wasn't hiding anything else, he told me to leave the room. I was in a hallway and was instructed to go up a metal staircase. The rusty iron stairs squeaked and groaned as I climbed them. At the top was a small hallway with two doors. One of them opened. I could now hear Tim without the phone.

"Drop the phone and stomp on it." He stuck his head out the door and watched me smash the phone to pieces.

"But I don't have insurance for my phone," I said, a lame joke. Anything to try and jog him out of his single-minded focus. *Focus on what?* was the question running around inside my head.

"Just do it! Then come in here."

The room was large, probably an old storage room. There were still a few boxes stacked around the edges. Taped to a chair in the middle of the room was Margret Devries. She had a gag over her mouth and her eyes were hot and hostile.

"So what do you know?" he asked in voice that was way too calm.

"I think I have most of it figured out."

"Sit down in that chair." He pointed to a chair at a ninety-degree angle from Margret's and about ten feet away.

"You're Mark Kemper's son," I said, sitting down in the chair.

He tossed me a roll of duct tape. "Tape your feet to the legs of the chair and then tape your left hand to the arm."

I started taping my feet. "I find it hard to understand why you had to kill him. I'm sure it was a shock, but..."

"He killed my real father!" he screamed. "First he tells him that ridiculous story that he had sex with her." He pointed to his mother. "He was gay! I know she's a whore, but how could he? How could *she*?" His fury was palpable. "An hour after Kemper left us, Dad collapsed. That queer killed my father and tried to convince me that I was his son."

I'd managed to tape up my feet and hand. He came over to me, his face flushed from the fury surging through him. When he went to grab the tape from my hand I hit him as hard as I could with my free hand. The angle and the leverage was all off. I made solid contact, but not the knockout blow that I needed.

Fuming, he kicked my chair, causing me to fall over backward. I hit my head hard enough to leave me seeing stars. Before I had a chance to recover, he'd jerked my free hand over to the arm of the chair and was wrapping it with duct tape. He didn't bother to right my chair. The pain and blood rushing to my head caused me to blackout.

"Wake up, you moron!" I heard through the dense fog swirling between my ears. *Where am I? And why do I feel so odd?* I asked myself. "Wake up, wake up!" I couldn't think with all that racket.

"Shut the hell up!" I screamed. The yelling stopped and I managed to open my eyes.

Everything came back at once. I tried to look around, but it was hard to turn my head since part of my body weight was resting on it. I rolled the chair so that I was lying on my back. My neck was unsupported, but at least I could look around. Tim was nowhere to be seen. Margret was glaring at me.

"Are you finally awake?" she sneered. "You're lucky I got my gag off, otherwise who knows when you would have woken up?"

"We'll see if that was good or bad luck," I said, tired of her annoying voice already.

"Go ahead, Mister Bruce Willis, make jokes. He's going to come back here and kill both of us."

I had to roll over on my side to give my neck some rest. Looking around the room, I couldn't see anything that would help me get the tape off my hands or feet. Both of us had tape wrapped around our hands as well as our wrists. Nothing dumb about Tim. Trying to scoot or roll myself and the chair was next to impossible. Finally, I lay still, exhausted and sore from my efforts.

"Do something!" she yelled at me.

"I don't see what I can do!" I yelled back, exasperated. "If you had told me that he was Mark Kemper's son right from the beginning, we wouldn't be in this situation."

"Screw you. I didn't know he'd killed Mark. And I can't believe he killed Dell." She sounded genuinely baffled.

"I doubt that he knew he was going to do it when he went to meet with her. But the revelation about his parentage and the shock of Jim Devries, the man he thought was his father, being struck down by a stroke. You add on the fact that he wasn't going to inherit a farm and a business that he'd dedicated his life to if the truth got out, his reaction is not that shocking." I paused. "Dell must have realized what had happened. I take it she knew that Mark was Tim's father?"

"I told her the truth when I learned I was pregnant. The two of us figured out that I could marry Jim and he'd never know any different. We'd had sex a couple of times, and he wasn't too smart about stuff like that."

"You took advantage of him."

"I gave him a hell of a lot. He loved marrying me. I was the catch of the county. You don't know how many men were panting after me."

"You had all those guys after you, then why the hell did you sleep with Mark?" My neck was killing me. I had to change position again.

"Ha! That was the first and only time I took pity on someone. See where it got me? Mark told me he thought he was gay. Queer, was the word he used. He was so young and pathetic. He was the first guy that I liked. Weird, right? It wasn't a sex thing. I'd just gone out with him 'cause he had the hot car, and he talked about something other than football. I was going to ditch him as soon as I got tired of riding around with him. But then he told me he might be gay and got all teary-eyed and sad. I looked over at him, curled up against the door of the car, and I told him there was one way to find out."

"Great, pity sex killed us. They can put that on our gravestones," I moaned.

"It wasn't good. He managed to get it hard and push it in. Boys being boys, his little man took over and finished the job. Afterward he cried."

"Wait a minute! You all did it by the old juke joint. That's why Tim picked the warehouse parking lot to kill Mark."

"I guess so."

"When did Mark know that Tim was his son?"

"I've always been a bitch. I told him I was pregnant. More crying. I couldn't stand the sight of him at that point and told him to go away and never talk to me again. I honestly thought he might have blocked it out of his memory. I guess he didn't." She said the last bit softly, as if she finally felt real regret.

I looked toward the door. "Where do you think Tim went?"

"Where do you think? Look around. Who's missing from our happy little family?" she asked bitterly.

"Tilly."

"We have a bingo. The only legitimate heir to the Devries name and property."

"Why didn't you tell me about Tim?"

"Jesus, are you that naïve? I thought I could work it to my advantage. Jim had a lot of money. I got a very small piece of the pie when we got divorced."

"But Tim killed your sister!"

"Guess I was in denial about that. Anyway, she was dead. Nothing was going to bring her back. What did Norman Bates say, 'we all go a little crazy sometimes'? I hoped he'd gotten it out of his system. Honestly, I thought your lot would find some evidence and arrest him. You didn't. And then he started asking a lot of questions."

"Questions?"

"About who else might know. Were there any records? That sort of thing."

"Let me guess, you told him about the doctor."

"Dr. Brook knew that it wasn't Jim's baby. He and Dell were the only ones. I told Tim that he might have some records that would give it away."

"So you didn't tell me that Tim was Mark's son, which would have saved lives, but you told Tim about Dr. Brook and got him killed. So why did Tim turn on you?"

She was quiet for a while. "I didn't like the way he was looking at me. I decided to make a run for it."

"He caught you?"

"I did the second decent thing in my life. I called Tilly to warn her. I got her voicemail and got part of the story out before he grabbed me and brought me here."

"But, wait, I'm still confused. If you had gotten Tim arrested for the murders, Tilly would have inherited. Wouldn't that have worked out for you?"

"Have you been living under a rock all your life? Mothers and daughters don't really get along that well. Every time I thought that might be the way to go, I remembered how many times I'd called her a fat pig. Or told her that a dress

185

would look better on a horse, or any number of not-so-sweet things I said. Even though Tim stayed with his father, he always called me. We had a little of the mother/son bonding thing going on. Right before he abducted me, I thought that I might have done the right thing by breastfeeding him. Guess it didn't make a difference."

There were sounds coming from the stairs—steps, struggling, creaky flooring and muffled screaming. The door opened and Tim shoved Tilly, taped up like the rest of us, into the room. She stumbled and fell, landing close to me. Her angry, terrified eyes looked into mine, pleading for help, but I couldn't give her any hope.

Tim closed the door and stood looking at all of us. No one said a word for a few moments, and then Margret and I spoke at once.

"I'd clap, but you taped my hands to the chair," Margret said. "You're getting quite the collection."

"Tim, you don't have to go down this road," I said. He stared at me with dead eyes. "We can resolve this. My father can help get you out of this bind."

My inner voice wanted to know why the hell I hadn't taken the hostage negotiation class at Quantico when it was offered. I'd had a choice—I could have gone to Virginia and learned to talk slowly and calmly about pleasant things to homicidal maniacs, or I could have gone to Shot Show in Las Vegas and looked at all the cool new weapons and body armor, plus gone to range day and shoot guns I could never afford to own. So I went to Las Vegas on the county dime with two other guys from our department. I should have at least gotten the notes for the FBI hostage class. A little late now.

"Tim, listen to me, please." All I got was a stare. He was looking at all of us slowly. Not good. I felt like a lobster in a tank at a seafood restaurant.

"I'm your mother," Margret started, but before she could say more he got right in her face and roared.

"I hate you! You've ruined my whole life. Every thing I

ever thought was true turned out to be a lie. Now I've done horrible things because of the lies you told me. I wish I could kill you a million times. Over and over and over again." He was miming hitting her with a blunt object. An appeal to motherly love wasn't going to get us very far.

I tried again. "Let's just talk this through. You and me. In fact, why don't you put duct tape over your mother's mouth?" This at least got him to look at me and smile a bit around the corners of his mouth.

"I should apologize for leaving you to listen to her bitchy voice. I don't have anything against you." That was a ray of light. Though I didn't think I'd get officer of the year if I talked him into freeing me and left his mom and sister to be killed.

"I understand how this all happened. Believe me, I've seen people get out of worse scrapes." That was a complete lie. No way was he going to "get out" of this mess. But I didn't know what else to say. I just hoped he was in shock and not seeing the obvious cluster he'd gotten himself into. After three murders and three kidnappings, I was perfectly willing to call it a win if he killed himself and we all lived.

"Call the sheriff's office. Call my dad. You know him. He'll be honest with you. You know that. No one in the county is a straighter shooter than Dad." That was all true, and I was also confident that Dad would lie, cheat or steal to get hostages out safely.

"I'm not calling anyone. I'm going to finish this here and now," he said in icy tones. Not good. We were approaching "nothing to lose" on the take-a-chance meter.

"Your real dad was gay?" I blurted out.

Tim came over and looked down into my face. "Don't say that," he said in a menacing voice. Tim and Jim were very religious. I knew that aspect of the situation had to be eating at him. By harping on it, was I going to help or was I lining myself up to die with the other two? What would Quantico say?

"Why not, it's the truth, right?" This earned me a kick in

the ass. His boot rammed into my butt three times before stopping.

"That's why I've got to kill everyone who knows. All of it is lies!" he shouted. I didn't point out the logical fallacy of that argument.

Margret, who'd remained silent since I suggested that Tim tape her mouth shut, had to step in. "Mark was your father. You'd better accept that. I know I did wrong not telling you a long time ago, but I thought I was doing it for your own good. Listen to me, I won't spill your secret. You can kill these two and I'll help you convince the cops that Tilly killed everyone." That last part caused Tilly to start kicking and squirming on the floor in anger. I just sent a very specific telepathic message to Margret: *You bitch!*

"Everyone knows that Jim was your father. No one is going to believe her."

"Don't bullshit me," he said angrily.

I tried another angle. "Okay, listen, you believe in God. What you've done is wrong. But you can make up for it. You have the chance to save three people's lives. Your dad, Jim, would have wanted that. He loved you. He loved Tilly. Hell, at one time he even loved your mom."

Tim looked at me with cold eyes. "After Mark told him I was his son, the son of a gay man and a woman that 'Jim' had learned to hate, do you know what 'Jim' did? He spat in my face and told me to pack my things and get out of his house. All my life I only wanted one thing, just one thing." He was down in my face now. "I wanted that man to be proud of me. Got up every morning determined to do whatever I had to do so that he would look at me with pride. When he introduced me to people as his son I could hear the pride in his voice. All of that was gone."

"Then Jim was wrong. Mark was a good man. Jim never should have put that on you. I'm sure he would have felt differently over time. Obviously he didn't know about any of this either. He was as shocked as you. Think how he must have felt. But you are a great son, and the fact that you all didn't share DNA wouldn't have mattered when he had time to think about it."

"None of this matters. We're beyond all of that. He's dead. Mark's dead. My aunt is dead."

I was waiting for him to add that we would be joining them soon enough. I knew I hadn't changed his mind at all. Tim was backed into a corner by fate and his own actions. He could only see one door. He only had one chance to get out of all of this—kill everyone.

CHAPTER TWENTY-TWO

"Redemption." I was straining to remember Sunday sermons and the few bible classes I'd attended. "As long as there is life, there is the chance for redemption. You can be forgiven."

For a moment he seemed to think about what I was saying. But then he turned and left the room. I relaxed. If he wasn't in the room, he couldn't kill us. My only strategy now was to stall for time. For what? I didn't know, but every second we were alive was a second more that we were alive.

"I don't think you're helping," Margret said with venom.

"Don't you even start. Trying to throw your own daughter and me under the bus. I get free, I'll club you to death myself."

Tim came back into the room and when I saw the hammer he was carrying, a shiver ran down my spine, a spine that was feeling various shades of yellow. I couldn't be sure, but in my heart I knew that it was the blunt object he'd used on Mark or Dell.

"Wait." He stopped and looked at me with those dead eyes as my mind searched for something, anything, to stall him. "At least take the gag off of Tilly."

His eyes narrowed. "Why would I do that?"

"She deserves to have her say."

"She deserves? How the hell do you figure she deserves anything? Not once did she ever think of Dad. Never. Always what she wanted. Don't tell me what she deserves."

"Let her speak. You've had your say. Let's hear what she has to say."

He looked exasperated. "I don't have to take that tape off. I'll tell you what she'll say. She's going to whine and cry and tell us how she's the victim."

"You really are afraid to give her a chance, aren't you?" I kept going. If he was talking, he wasn't bashing—that was my new motto.

"Fine. You have got to be the stupidest…" He went over and ripped, literally ripped, the tape off of her mouth. She would never have to worry about hair on that upper lip.

She screamed and kept screaming.

"You happy?" he asked, looking at me.

"Shut up. Hey, Tilly," I said, trying to get her attention. "Talk to him!" I yelled over her screaming.

"Turn me loose! Help! Help!" she continued to screech. Running out of breath, she panted and began to calm down some. "Damn it, Tim, let me go!"

"No."

"Tim, pleaaaaseeee."

"That shit worked on Dad. Not on me. I saw through every one of your little ploys. You always got your way without lifting a finger. You'd do some stupid crap and he'd give you money or buy you a new car. You're the one that should have been kicked out of the family. Hell, you left and he forgave you."

Tim raised the hammer and moved toward her. She cringed and tried to scoot away. She must have seen the same look I saw in his eyes.

"What are you going to do, kill all of us?" I asked, trying to redirect his attention.

"Yes." For a minute I thought he was going to swing the hammer.

"Then what? Tim, what are you going to do then?" I shouted this, trying to take his focus off of his sister.

Again he hesitated. "I'll get rid of your bodies and go on living my life."

"That's not how it's going to work. Do you think my dad is going to give up until he's found the person who murdered me?"

"No one's going to find your body. Or theirs," he said, pointing the hammer at the women.

"Where are you going to dump us? That old sinkhole on your property?" This surprised him. He turned back to me, and I knew that I'd guessed right. "The most obvious body dump around? Please. They'll be dragging that before Christmas. You'd better come up with a cleverer plan than that."

He was staring at me now, hefting the hammer up and down.

I looked around. There was only one dirty window in the room. I momentarily fantasized that Pete was out there somewhere with a rifle trained on Tim.

"Maybe I can help you. The coast is only about an hour away. You could do the Dexter thing and chop us up and sink us out at sea."

"Shut up!" Tilly yelled. "What are you doing?"

What you wouldn't do; engaging him in conversation, I thought. But I ignored her and kept eye contact with Tim. I was exhausted and sore, but determined to drag this out as long as possible. I wanted to get every last second out of my life.

"No, you'd be sure to get a ton of trace evidence in any vehicle you used. Besides, you'd have to rent a boat, which means there would be a record of it. Must be a better way."

Tim was staring at me. I seemed to have him mesmerized. "Okay, sinkhole out, dumping at sea out. Burning! That's it!"

"Don't help him! Stop it!" Tilly screamed.

"Shut up!" Margret yelled at Tilly. "Just shut the hell up. My God, you are the whiniest daughter any woman ever had.

Tim, you and I can agree to that. Don't you think for one minute I was happy when she said she'd go with me. I wanted you to come live with me. Like you said, you had a work ethic. She never did one damn thing to help me. Always take, take, take."

Tim turned on her now. I think Margret understood what we had to do, or she was just looking for another opportunity to sell us out.

"Where do you think she learned it?" Tim demanded. "From you! I should have killed you before. Every time you called Dad on the phone wanting some shit, he'd go into a funk for days. He wanted to tell you no, but he couldn't. That stupid old man loved you even after you tore his heart out. That's why you never told him the truth. Finding out that you tricked him into taking care of a bastard child would have been the last straw. He would have kicked you to the curb if he'd have known that your whole marriage had been built on a lie. Nothing was real."

He swung the hammer, but pulled the punch at the last second, hitting Margret on the side of the head. I didn't think it was a death blow. Margret screamed, and when she tried to avoid the hammer's second swing, her chair toppled. The other side of her head bounced off the floor. She lay there dazed and whimpering.

I could see that his actions had sent adrenaline coursing through Tim's system. He was pacing up and down, swinging the hammer and mumbling, working himself up to kill one of us. At that moment I heard a noise. Someone or something was on the staircase. At this point I didn't care what it was. I yelled for help. I screamed.

They came through the door like champions. Smoke filled the room and there were people shouting. Thrown to the floor, Tim roared with rage like a trapped animal. A hand grabbed me. Through the haze of smoke and confusion, I saw my father dressed in tactical gear, kneeling beside me.

"Are you okay?"

I had to think about it for a minute. "Sure," I answered.

He lifted the chair into an upright position. Pulling a knife out, he started cutting away the tape. Matt had Tim on the ground, handcuffing him. Pete, wearing a tac vest several sizes too small for him, came lumbering in and over to me.

"They had me posted on the other building or I'd have been with the entry team."

"Hell, we'd have used you as a battering ram," Dad said and then turned to me. "What is going on?"

"Tim killed them all." The look in his eyes told me that he'd had no idea.

"If you didn't know that, why are you here? How'd you find me?" I asked, puzzled.

Dad took out his phone and started going through it. "Your girlfriend called us. Lucky for you, she isn't stupid. After half an hour of waiting, she went looking for you. Not finding you or the car, and not getting any answer when she called your cell phone, she decided she better call someone. She called the vet, got my personal number and told me that she thought something had happened to you. We put out the alarm. Had everybody looking for your car or you. Then we found your car parked in the Supersave lot." I realized Tim must have moved it when he went out looking for Tilly.

"About an hour ago, I got a text that gave this address with 911 and your name. We came up slowly, caught a glimpse of Tim at the window and thought that you might be inside. We were working on a plan when we heard the scream."

"Funny. I didn't send you a text," I told him.

He looked at me and raised his eyebrows. "Well, doesn't matter, I guess. You must have a guardian angel. I'll leave it to you to figure out how to write up that part of the report. In my after-action report, I'm just going to put that we received an anonymous tip."

He put his hand out to help me out of the chair. Every muscle in my body was aching. Margret and Tilly were already being led down the stairs.

"Wait a minute," I called to the officers leading Margret down. "After she's been checked out at the hospital, I want her brought to the jail and put into a holding cell."

She turned, her face beet red. "What are you talking about? I'm going to sue you and everyone in this backwoods sheriff's office."

"Have at it. But I'm going to do my best to get the State Attorney to prosecute you as an accessory to at least one, if not two, of the murders." Her face went from red to ashen white. The men on either side of her had to catch her to keep her from collapsing.

I filled Dad in on all the details as he drove me home.

"I don't understand why he went to the trouble of cutting off Kemper's fingers and smashing his face. He must have known we'd figure out who Kemper was."

"I think he was in such a daze after killing him that he wasn't thinking. The face probably had more to do with suppressed rage than an attempt to cover up the identity of the body. The hands might have been part of a half-thought out plan. The shock of having killed him was so overwhelming that Tim probably convinced himself he could get away with it. Then, when no one arrested him and we didn't identify Mark right away, he realized that other people knew and had to be dealt with."

Dad stayed with me for an hour and then left me to decompress with Ivy's cuddly attention. Around nine o'clock I decided to call Cara. I wanted to let her know I was all right, how grateful I was, and how sorry I was for the way the day had turned out.

"Larry, I'm so glad you weren't hurt."

"Thanks to you."

"I kind of figured something was wrong. You don't strike me as the type of guy to run out on a date like that."

"Not usually. Funny, when all of this was going down, I kept worrying about how mad you must be."

195

"I'll admit that when I got out to the parking lot I had a moment when I thought you might be the biggest asshole I've ever gone out with. But when I thought about you…." She paused. "Well, I couldn't believe that. Of course, my other uncharitable idea was that you'd had some sort of psychotic break."

"That could happen at any time," I joked.

"Larry." She got quiet, then went on solemnly, "I'm not sure the dating thing is going to work."

"But you know I didn't skip—"

"Not that. I know you didn't have any choice but to leave me. I just don't think the cop thing works for me."

I answered sincerely, "I'm not married to this job. I know guys who are. I'm not."

"I believe you. But it's too soon for me to know how I feel about you. So I can't ask you to give it up right now. Besides, I don't think you're ready to abandon your father." There was no malice in her tone.

"I wouldn't be abandoning him."

"I think he might feel like you were, and you might too." Deep down I knew she might be right.

"We're still friends?"

"Of course."

"If I bump into you somewhere, we can chat like old school chums."

"Yes."

"You'll leave the door open to the possibility that in the future we might date again?"

"Yes, I will. As long as you promise not to run out and leave me with the bill again."

"That's a deal."

We said our goodbyes. I was staring at the phone feeling sorry for myself when it rang. The caller ID said "CI."

"Eddie, what can I do for you?" I asked, perhaps a little more curtly than was polite.

"That's it? 'What can I do for you?'" he said, sounding perturbed.

"It's late and I've had a rough day."

"Your day might have been a lot rougher if I hadn't texted your daddy where you were."

"*You* did that?"

"I heard you were missing. Told you I was keeping my ear to the ground. Not hard with the cops in the family. Then I thought they might want to check out the address where a guy told my friend he'd met a fellow who was interested in starting fires."

"Damn."

"Yeah, sounds a little better having me as an informant now, doesn't it?" He was clearly enjoying his victory lap.

"Yeah, Eddie, I guess it does." I had to give him that.

"Right, next time maybe you'll answer my text."

"Promise. Thanks, I mean it. Thanks."

"No problem. Catch you later." And he hung up.

Terrific. My relationship with my confidential informant rat was going fine, but I'd somehow buggered up my chance at romance.

"Ivy, I think you are going to be due for a trip to the vet in a few weeks." Ivy only looked at me with her *we'll see about that* stare.

Larry Macklin returns in:

December's Secrets
A Larry Macklin Mystery–Book 2

Here's a preview:

The winds of December were bringing in frigid air. High humidity and low temperatures can deliver bone-chilling cold, even in north Florida. Shivering a bit, I watched the crime scene techs try to cut the corpse from the tree without damaging any evidence that might have been on the rope it hung from.

Uncharitably, I was glad that the man was white. I really didn't want to deal with all the racial connotations that would come if the victim had been black. The corpse was wearing cargo pants, cheap hiking boots and a plaid shirt over a long-sleeve undershirt. From what I could see from the ground, he looked to be in his mid-thirties. His hair was brown and uncut. His swollen facial features made it hard to tell much more about him. The body had been discovered earlier this morning after dispatch received an anonymous tip.

Shantel Williams and Marcus Brown, two of our Adams County crime techs, were being assisted by three more from the Florida Department of Law Enforcement. Since we're a small county of less than thirty thousand, we often call on FDLE to assist us with major crimes. Having Tallahassee in the next county over had its advantages.

They had rigged up a second rope so they could cut the rope used for the hanging, but still be able to lower the body gently to the ground. A van from the coroner's office was waiting to take it to the morgue in Tallahassee.

"Be careful now. No need breaking any bones that aren't already broken," Shantel told the guys who were lowering the body. The mocha-skinned middle-aged woman took charge of any situation she found herself in. And when things went wrong, even when it was no fault of her own, she was the first one to take the blame.

A few minutes after the body was placed on the ground, she came over to me holding the dead man's wallet open in her gloved hand so that I could read the information on his driver's license. "At least you won't have to waste time trying to figure out who he is," she said.

"Very considerate of him to keep his wallet with him during his brutal execution," I told her.

"Don't be a smartass. It's too cold for that. You know I'm supposed to be Christmas shopping this morning? I had the day off. Esther and I had the whole day planned... Going to go to Tallahassee and shop until we dropped. But you all just had to find a dead body. Out in these woods, it could have hung here for another day without someone finding it," Shantel said, shaking her head. "You think Marcus is going to be happy? Esther is *not* going to be in a good mood."

Marcus and Shantel worked together almost every day and Marcus's wife, Esther, was Shantel's best friend. Hey, it was a small town and an even smaller sheriff's department. Though I knew she didn't want to hear it now, I was glad they had called her in. Marcus and Shantel were the best crime scene techs in the department.

While Shantel ranted on about having to come in to work, I wrote down the man's name and vitals: 5'10", 200 pounds, brown eyes, brown hair. Doug Timberlane. The name didn't ring any bells with me.

Looking over at our unmarked car, I could see my partner, Pete Henley, texting furiously on his phone. Considering the size of the big man's chubby fingers, he always impressed me with his dexterity. "Pete!" I yelled. He continued texting. "Pete, put your damn phone away and come over here."

He typed for another second, apparently hit "send" and

looked up. "You don't have teenage daughters." He brought his three-hundred-plus pounds to an upright position and came lumbering over to me.

"Ever hear of a Doug Timberlane?" I asked.

"That him?" He pointed to the body.

"No, I'm pulling random names out of my ass to ask you about."

"He's in one of his smartass moods," Shantel said while she bagged and tagged the wallet.

"No. There are some Timberlys that live north of town, but I can't say I know any Timberlanes," Pete said. I made fun of him, but Pete had an encyclopedic knowledge of the people and the history of Adams County. I had seen him solve more than one case simply by making connections between people, their families and their friends.

"According to his wallet, he lives on Sawgrass Road in the north end of the county," I told him.

"There are quite a few trailers and old houses for rent out that way."

I knew the area because of frequent calls for service when I was on the road. There were plenty of domestic abuse and overdose calls and all the other crimes that went with unemployment, poverty and substance abuse.

"If you'll keep an eye on things here I'll ride up there. Maybe I can find some family or friends," I said to Pete, who was checking his phone again. "Only if you can tear yourself away from your messages."

"Yeah, yeah. Go, I got this," Pete said good-naturedly.

I turned the heat up as I drove out on the dirt road that led back to the main highway. The murder site appeared more secluded than it actually was. Go a hundred yards any direction, you'd run into a neighborhood. We were just south of Calhoun, the county seat. I knew a woman who lived not too far away. We had dated a couple times and I still had hopes that it might become a real relationship. Unfortunately, she wasn't comfortable getting involved with a sheriff's deputy.

I thought about driving by Cara's duplex, but decided that would be too stalkerish. I headed on into town, going through a dozen or so stoplights and passing the large courthouse in the square. The car bounced over the railroad tracks that still divided Calhoun into the haves and the have-nots. I drove past the warehouse parking lot where a murder had recently taken place. I'd gotten lucky solving the case. I'd gotten lucky *surviving* the case.

Fifteen minutes later I turned onto Sawgrass Road and began checking numbers on houses and mailboxes. It was a challenge in this rundown area. Many of the numbers were missing or impossible to read. When I finally found Timberlane's address, I was looking at a mobile home that was at least twenty years old, faded and neglected. Pulling up in the driveway, it was obvious that this guy was not a high roller. The grass in the yard hadn't been cut for months and was brown and dry from the recent frosts.

There was an old pickup in the driveway. When I called in the tag, it came back registered to a David Tyler. We hadn't found any vehicles close to the site of the hanging, so I didn't know if Timberlane had a car or not. This could have certainly been his truck—he wouldn't be the first poor guy who didn't have the money to get all the paperwork right on his vehicle. I looked in the windows and saw the front seat was covered in fast food bags and cups, discarded cigarette packs and other trash. Nothing unusual or helpful—no bloodstains or the other half of the rope he was hung with.

I climbed the trailer's rickety wooden stairs and knocked on the door. No answer. I walked around to the back door. No luck there either. But I spotted an old man sitting on the screened porch of the equally dilapidated home next door. I waved and he took a hand out from underneath a pile of blankets to wave back.

"Kind of cold to be sitting outside," I shouted to him.

"Fresh air. Gotta have my air," he answered in a voice gravelly from too much smoking and drinking.

I walked next door. "Can I ask you a few questions?"

"You a repo man?"

I took out my bi-fold and held up my star. "Deputy."

"Sure, come on up."

It was always refreshing to meet a member of the public that was willing to talk to law enforcement. His porch looked like it had been built with scavenged wood. I walked up the stairs and opened the door very carefully, afraid that it might just fall off. The old man was seated in a rocker. Up close, I decided that he probably wasn't much over fifty, but a life lived rough had taken its toll.

"Have a seat. I'd stand up, but I just got warm." He smiled at me. The man had fewer teeth than I had fingers.

"I'm Deputy Larry Macklin." Since his hands were under the blankets, I didn't offer to shake.

"Macklin? I thought you was the sheriff."

"That's my father, Ted Macklin," I said. I'd had to explain the relationship between my father and me at least a million times over the years.

"Oh, gotcha, I'm Jeremy Wright. Nice to meet cha'."

"Do you know your neighbor?" I nodded toward the house next door.

"Oh, yeah. That rascal moved in about two months ago. Can't say I'm surprised that a cop is interested in him."

"Why's that?"

"Mean as a snake, a thief, most likely a rapist and an ex-con." He said all of this with great conviction.

"You seem pretty sure."

"I know his type. I've been in prison a couple times myself. Not for nothin' but drugs and drunk fighting. It's not hard to tell the bad ones. And he's a bad one. Had run-ins with a couple of the folks around here."

"About what?" I took out my pad and pen.

"Tom up the street had a chainsaw go missing. And the Alarcons, they ain't from here, the mister got in a fight with

Timberlane about him making comments to his daughter. And she's only fourteen."

"When was this?"

"Not long after Timberlane moved in."

"Any problems since then?"

"What's this all about? He hurt someone?"

"Just the opposite. Someone killed him."

"Good! If I was younger, I'd have roughed him up myself. Never killed no one, but I'd have liked to beat the snot out of that SOB."

"Did he have trouble with anyone else?"

"Now I don't know if I want to help no more. I thought I'd be getting him in trouble and that was all right. Someone killed Timberlane, and he needed killing, well, I don't know if I want to put the heat on them or not."

I thought for a moment what the best approach would be. "What I've learned is that, if a bad guy gets killed, it's most often another bad guy that did it."

He leaned back and thought about it. Finally he said, "True. Well, there was a guy yesterday got in a big fight with Timberlane right in the front yard."

My heart beat a little faster. Maybe this was going to be one of the easy ones. "What did the man look like? Did you know him?"

"Nah, never seen him before. I'd remember if I did. Big old horse of a man. More 'an six feet, maybe six and a half, and no bean pole neither."

"How old was he?"

"Mid-fifties, maybe? Had a ponytail hanging down his back."

"What color was his hair?"

"Light, blondish, think there was some grey in it."

"What kind of clothes was he wearing?"

"What I'd call working man's. Flannel shirt and jean overalls. Nothing new. They were kinda dirty. Oh, yeah, big old work boots."

"Did he come in a car?"

"Older crew cab pickup, think it was a Chevy. Grey. Kind of beat up."

"Didn't happen to see the tag, did you?"

"Nope." Of course I couldn't be that lucky.

"Any other markings on the truck?"

"Not that I saw."

"What did they argue about?"

"Funny about that. They were having like two arguments. On the one hand, Timberlane was all mad about not getting a check or something about being paid, and the big man was mad about some girl."

We needed to backtrack. "Okay, let's start from the beginning. Where were you, and how did this fight start?"

"I was sitting out here. Little warmer yesterday. Anyway, this man, the big one, pulled up in Timberlane's driveway. He got out, went up and knocked on the door. Just like you. Only Timberlane was home. Door opens and the big man stepped back into the yard like he didn't want to go in the house. Timberlane come down and asked something about his money that was owed him. The big man, he pulled out an envelope and tossed it on the ground. Timberlane didn't take too kindly to that. He told him to pick it up. Big man said 'eff you.' Told Timberlane that if he ever saw him again it'd mean a trip to the hospital for Timberlane. Timberlane asked him what his problem was. Big guy says he ought to have Timberlane charged with rape.

"You could see that the big guy was getting more worked up. I thought I was going to see Timberlane get his ass whipped for sure. But I guess he saw the same thing I did. Timberlane said 'screw you' and picked up the envelope, tore it open and looked at what was inside. He shot the big man a bird, but he was backing up toward the house at the same time. Big man just stood there. Then said that if he ever saw Timberlane again he'd do some permanent damage to him. That's the words he used, permanent damage."

"Then the big guy left?"

"Yeah. But he stood outside watching the house for a

couple more minutes after Timberlane went inside. Like he was thinking about doing more. But, yeah, he went back to his truck and drove off real fast."

"Nothing else you can remember?"

"No, don't think so."

I got the names and addresses of the other neighbors who'd had encounters with Timberlane, gave Mr. Wright my card and thanked him for his help.

"Don't mind at all. I'm just glad someone got rid of that asshole. Honestly, part of me hopes you don't catch him."

I talked to a couple of the other neighbors and got the same impression of Doug Timberlane. The consensus was that the world was a better place for him being strung up in a tree. I wondered if he had family that might feel differently. I called Pete and got him working on tracking down the owner of the trailer. I needed to get inside and search it. But that could wait. I headed back to the crime scene.

The body had been hauled off by the time I got back. Pete had called in some off-duty deputies and some of our civilian employees to help our crime scene techs search the area for any other evidence.

I caught up with Shantel and she took me to the dead man's effects. I asked her to go ahead and dust his cell phone. After she'd lifted several prints, she handed it to me. Checking it, I saw a number for "Mom." I pressed it.

"David?"

That was weird, but then I remembered the registration of the truck in Timberlane's driveway. I impressed myself by thinking on my feet for a change. "No, I found this phone. I saw the 'Mom' number and thought I might be able to get it back to its rightful owner. Is this David's phone?"

No answer. "Hello?"

There was more dead air and then the connection was broken. Apparently I wasn't fooling anybody. I pushed the button again. She answered but didn't say anything.

"Look, I'm a deputy with the Adams County, Florida Sheriff's Office. You may as well talk to me because if you don't, I'm simply going to use this number to find you."

She said nothing for half a minute, but she didn't disconnect either. Finally, "How'd you get this phone?" The voice was soft and downcast. This was a person who was used to getting bad news.

"I was telling the truth. I found it. Could you give me your name, please?" I had my pad and pen out and leaned on the hood of my car to write.

"Tammy Page. Where did you find it?" A tremor came into her voice.

"Do you have a son, Ms. Page?"

"Yes. Is David all right? Please, is he okay?" Desperation and something else. I think she had been expecting this call for a long time.

"I don't know. We found the phone, but it was in the possession of someone by the name of Doug Timberlane."

"Is he okay?" She was almost yelling now. She hadn't asked who Doug Timberlane was, which led me to one conclusion. I'm not always very good at this detection thing so maybe I was wrong, but it was worth a shot.

"Does your son use the name Doug Timberlane sometimes?"

The question got more of the silent treatment.

"Ms. Page, where do you live?"

"Orlando."

"Is anyone with you?"

"Oh, my God. No! Tell me he's okay. Please." She began to cry.

"Ms. Page, we found the body of a man. The license in his wallet identified him as Doug Timberlane."

She was just wailing now. There was no point in going on. I told her that I would call back in an hour and hung up.

"Apparently this might not be Doug Timberlane," I said to Shantel. She pulled the dead man's wallet out of the evidence case and we took it apart, dusting the cards and money carefully.

"That answers one question," I said, holding up his license. While it was inside the plastic sleeve it looked real enough to fool me, but without the plastic to obscure the flaws, it was obviously a fake.

There was one card in an interior pocket bearing the name David Tyler. "I think we have a winner. Mom thought it was David calling, and the truck in the driveway was registered to a David Tyler."

Pete and his crew came up with a plastic bin of bagged items that they'd found scattered over an acre around the murder scene. Most of it—cigarette butts, old potato chip bags and odds and ends of clothing—would prove useless. But there was one interesting item—a pay-as-you-go cell phone. If we could find out who purchased it and where, we just might find our killer.

ACKNOWLEDGMENTS

Many thanks to my beta readers—Chuck Mitchell, Jan Lydon, Judy Sutton and Locke Haney—for reading the story and providing lots of positive feedback and edits.

I never would have had the courage to attempt self-publishing without the constant support and encouragement of H. Y. Hanna. She has provided an endless supply of valuable lists, resources and advice. She was invaluable as a beta reader and developed a great cover design for the series. Words cannot express my appreciation for all her help.

Good fortune smiled on me when I met a woman who could be my friend, my editor and my wife. Many things in my life, including this series, could not be accomplished without Melanie by my side.

Original Cover Design by H. Y. Hanna
Paperback Cover Design by Robin Ludwig Design Inc.
www.gobookcoverdesign.com

ABOUT THE AUTHOR

A. E. Howe lives and writes on a farm in the wilds of north Florida with his wife, horses and more cats than he can count. He received a degree in English Education from the University of Georgia and is a produced screenwriter and playwright. His first published book was *Broken State*; the Larry Macklin Mysteries is his first series and he has plans for more. Howe is also the co-host of the "Guns of Hollywood" podcast, part of the Firearms Radio Network. When not writing or podcasting, Howe enjoys riding, competitive shooting and working on the farm.